Crimson Intrigue

Nina Hill

Published by Nina Hill, 2024.

This is a work of fiction. Similarities to real people, places, or events are entirely coincidental.

CRIMSON INTRIGUE

First edition. October 29, 2024.

Copyright © 2024 Nina Hill.

ISBN: 979-8227567642

Written by Nina Hill.

Chapter 1: A Glimpse Through Glass

The moon hung low in the indigo sky, casting a silver sheen over the city that pulsed with life beneath it. I leaned against the cool glass of my office window, fingers splayed across the surface as if to steady myself against the dizzying height of our thirty-seventh floor. Below, the streets teemed with the hurried footsteps of people chasing their dreams, oblivious to the storm that brewed above their heads. Little did they know, I was caught in a whirlwind of my own, a tempest fueled by the looming threat of Mason Steele.

From my perch, I could see him clearly—his silhouette sharp against the glow of the skyline, a formidable figure with an air of confidence that seemed to bend the very atmosphere around him. The whispers in the boardroom had warned me of his arrival, a presence that could make or break fortunes in a single breath. But I wasn't here to quail before the great Mason Steele; I was here to protect my family's legacy, the small bakery my parents had nurtured like a fragile flower in a bustling concrete garden.

As I watched him, my heart thudded in a rhythm of defiance and fear. The bakery was more than just a business; it was a tapestry woven from the flour-dusted hands of my mother and the steady guidance of my father. It held the warmth of countless memories, from the smell of fresh bread wafting through our modest kitchen to the laughter of customers who had become friends. I could picture the quaint little shop with its cheerful awning and the tantalizing scent of pastries drawing in passersby. Every item on the menu told a story, and I was determined to keep those stories alive.

"Maya, you coming or what?" my colleague Jenna called out, breaking through my reverie. She was the kind of friend who pulled you into the chaos of life with her infectious laughter and vibrant energy. I turned away from the window, letting out a long breath, as if releasing the weight of the world.

"Just taking a moment," I replied, smoothing my blouse and stepping away from the seductive call of the night outside. Jenna rolled her eyes, a playful smirk dancing on her lips.

"Moments can wait, darling. Mason Steele is here! You know how much we could use a bit of his charm in this dull office? Come on, let's see if he's as handsome as they say."

With an exaggerated sigh, I followed her into the main lobby where the air buzzed with anticipation. Mason was mingling with the elite—his sharp suit sculpting his athletic frame, eyes glinting with that enigmatic spark that drew people in like moths to a flame. I was neither a moth nor a fan, but the draw of danger had its own allure. I stayed close to Jenna, half-dreading and half-curious about the man whose name sent ripples through the local economy.

As we approached, I overheard snippets of conversation, laughter echoing off the walls, but all I could focus on was him—the way he held court with a magnetic presence, effortlessly charming everyone around him. I wondered what he would do if he knew about the tiny bakery teetering on the brink of ruin, its foundation threatened by corporate expansion and his relentless ambition. Would he still smile that disarming smile, or would the storm clouds gather in his stormy gray eyes?

"Maya!" Jenna's voice cut through my thoughts. I realized she had made her way to the front, her enthusiasm drawing me into the fray. "Mason, this is Maya, our star project manager! She's practically the glue that holds our team together."

He turned, his gaze sweeping over me like a gentle breeze that raised goosebumps on my skin. A flicker of recognition danced in his eyes, but it was gone before I could analyze it. "Pleasure to meet you, Maya," he said, his voice low and smooth, like honey drizzled over warm bread.

"Likewise," I replied, forcing a smile, my heart racing against the backdrop of my mounting anxiety. The world around us faded; the laughter, the music, all diminished in importance as I faced the man who represented everything I feared.

"So, you're the one behind those successful projects we keep hearing about," he continued, his interest genuine, or at least feigned so well I couldn't discern the truth. "What's your secret?"

"Just a love for what I do," I said, my voice steady despite the turmoil inside. "And a determination not to let anyone—especially not tycoons—take away what my family built." I couldn't help the defiance that laced my words, an unintentional challenge hanging in the air between us.

His lips twitched at the corners, amusement flickering in his eyes. "That's a bold stance, especially in this city. It's a tough place for dreamers like you."

"Dreamers need to fight for their dreams," I shot back, an edge of steel in my tone, surprising myself with the conviction. "And I intend to do just that."

The room seemed to hold its breath, the electricity of our confrontation palpable. Around us, the chatter faded into the background, and for a moment, it felt like the world had shrunk to just the two of us—his dark allure and my determined spirit colliding in an unexpected duel.

His smile broadened, and there was something about it, a hint of respect mixed with intrigue. "I admire your spirit, Maya. Just don't get burned in the process."

With that, he turned back to the crowd, leaving me reeling, adrenaline coursing through my veins. I watched as he effortlessly mingled, charm cascading from him like confetti, but behind that facade, I felt the weight of his ambition lurking—a reminder that in this game of power, the stakes were higher than I had ever imagined.

Determined to keep my head above water, I swore to myself that I wouldn't let Mason Steele's shadow loom over my family's legacy. I had the heart of a fighter, and if there was one thing I knew, it was how to bake resilience into every loaf of bread.

The week dragged on like molasses, each day merging into the next, thick with the tension of unspoken challenges and half-formed plans. I threw myself into my work, pouring over spreadsheets and proposals as if they could shield me from the impending doom of Mason Steele's encroachment. In the mornings, I would awaken to the familiar aroma of freshly baked pastries wafting through my apartment, a gentle reminder of home. I would close my eyes and savor that scent, allowing it to anchor me before I stepped into the storm that awaited me.

By Thursday, the air felt charged with a strange mix of anxiety and anticipation. I could almost taste the impending confrontation. Jenna was relentless in her attempts to pry into my mind, her cheerful disposition clashing sharply with my brooding thoughts. "You need to stop overthinking everything," she insisted, tapping a finger against my desk as if trying to drum some sense into me. "Just go in there and be yourself. Maybe you'll charm him into reconsidering his plans."

"Charm him?" I scoffed, rolling my eyes. "I don't think charm will save my bakery from being bulldozed by the likes of Mason Steele. He's got the power of a freight train and the conscience of a gnat."

"Sounds like a challenge. Just think of it as a game of chess," she said, a mischievous glint in her eyes. "And you, my friend, are a queen. Use your power. You can't let him think you're intimidated. Stand tall. Show him you're the one in control."

"Right, because when I think of control, I picture a bakery owner challenging a corporate giant to a duel," I retorted, but deep down, her words lodged themselves in my thoughts like stubborn dough refusing to rise.

Later that evening, I found myself at home, surrounded by the warm glow of string lights and the comforting chaos of my kitchen. Flour dust danced in the air as I meticulously measured ingredients for the next day's batch of blueberry muffins. Baking was my sanctuary, a place where I could transform raw elements into something beautiful and, more importantly, delicious. As I mixed, the familiar rhythm soothed my racing heart, but the looming specter of Mason Steele hovered like a dark cloud.

I could hear my mother's voice in my head, a gentle reminder that good things take time and perseverance. She had often said, "You can't rush the dough, and you can't rush life." But time felt like a luxury I could no longer afford, especially with a corporate shark circling my family's legacy.

The next day, I was jolted from my thoughts by an unexpected notification on my phone. It was an email from the city council, informing me of a public meeting scheduled for the following week. They were discussing plans for new developments in the area, including a potential partnership with Mason Steele's company. My heart raced as I read through the details, each line a reminder of how dire the situation had become.

"Maya, you okay?" Jenna asked, her voice cutting through my spiraling thoughts. I glanced up to see her standing in the doorway, concern etched across her features.

"Just received some unsettling news," I murmured, my voice barely above a whisper. "It's about the council meeting. They're considering his proposal. If he gets the green light, the bakery... It could be the end."

"Then we'll fight," she declared, her determination radiating like sunlight breaking through clouds. "We'll gather support, rally the community. You know how much people love your bakery. They wouldn't let it go without a fight."

A flicker of hope ignited within me. The thought of standing up for my family's legacy alongside my friends and loyal customers gave me the strength I needed. "You're right," I said, lifting my chin with renewed vigor. "I need to speak up. This is my chance to show them I won't back down."

That night, I strategized my approach for the meeting, crafting a speech that combined heartfelt memories of my family's journey with hard facts about the economic impact of losing a small business. I practiced in front of my kitchen mirror, my hands animated as I spoke to my reflection.

The day of the meeting dawned, and I stood before the gathering crowd in the town hall, my heart pounding like a drum. The atmosphere buzzed with tension, the community packed tightly into the room, their expressions ranging from curiosity to outright concern. Mason Steele was there, of course, sitting at the front with an air of confidence that contrasted sharply with my own simmering anxiety.

"Thank you all for coming," I began, my voice trembling slightly but gaining strength with each word. "Today, I stand not just as a business owner but as a proud daughter of this community. My parents poured their hearts into our bakery, and it has become a gathering place for laughter, warmth, and memories."

As I spoke, I caught Mason's gaze. There was something unreadable in his expression, a mix of interest and amusement that made my stomach churn. I pushed on, recounting stories of customers who had shared milestones with us, the regulars who had become like family.

"The bakery isn't just a store; it's a symbol of resilience and passion," I concluded, my heart racing as I felt the weight of their eyes upon me. "I urge you to consider the value of keeping small businesses alive. We enrich this community. We matter."

As I finished, applause erupted around me, a wave of sound that surged through the room, fueling my confidence. But before I could bask in the glow of success, Mason rose from his seat. The atmosphere shifted, a palpable tension hanging in the air like smoke before a storm.

"I appreciate your sentiments, Maya," he said, his voice smooth as silk, "but let's not forget the potential for growth and progress that comes with development."

A collective murmur swept through the crowd, but I held my ground, ready for his calculated moves. "And let's not forget the heart of this community, Mason," I shot back, my tone sharper than I intended. "You can't build a city on concrete and steel alone. It requires soul."

The clash between us felt electric, a duel of wills played out in front of an audience eager for drama. I could see the flicker of surprise in his eyes, a moment of genuine admiration before his expression shifted back to that practiced, charming smile.

"Touché," he replied, his amusement barely concealed. "But a city needs to evolve, and sometimes that means letting go."

I sensed the underlying threat in his words, the reminder that he was still a formidable opponent. But as I stood before the audience, the support of my community bolstering my resolve, I felt a flicker of hope. Perhaps I could navigate this battlefield after all, using my heart and spirit as my armor.

The tension in the room felt palpable, an electric charge that crackled in the air as Mason Steele spoke. His voice, smooth and authoritative, wove through the crowd like a finely tailored suit. I had expected confrontation, perhaps even disdain, but instead, he had offered me an opportunity—a chance to reframe my argument, to find common ground in this relentless tug-of-war between progress and preservation.

"I appreciate your passion for your business, Maya," he continued, his tone almost congenial, "but let's be honest. The bakery, as lovely as it may be, is just a small piece of a much larger puzzle. Development is essential for growth, for the future of our city."

His words hung in the air, a mixture of truth and challenge. I could sense the crowd's ambivalence; many were torn between their affection for my bakery and the undeniable allure of new businesses, shiny and promising. I clenched my fists at my sides, rallying my thoughts. "And what future are you envisioning, Mason?" I shot back, my voice steady despite the whirlwind inside me. "One where every block is lined with towering glass buildings? Where the soul of this city is traded for corporate profits?"

A murmur of agreement rippled through the audience, and for a brief moment, I felt a surge of confidence. Mason's gaze narrowed slightly, a flicker of irritation flaring beneath his polished exterior. "Soul can be redefined, you know. Just as easily as buildings can be erected. I'm offering progress, not erasure."

"Progress doesn't have to come at the expense of our history," I replied, the heat of conviction flowing through me. "People don't just want to live in a city; they want to feel a connection to it. Our bakery is a part of that tapestry. It's about memories and warmth, something that no steel beam can replicate."

He chuckled, but there was an edge to it, a faint trace of irritation that hinted at the rivalry simmering between us. "You're a formidable opponent, I'll give you that. But don't underestimate the power of a fresh start."

His words danced dangerously close to a threat, igniting a fire in my belly. "And don't underestimate the resilience of a community. We're not just going to sit back and watch you bulldoze our lives. We will fight for what we believe in."

As the meeting progressed, I felt a renewed sense of determination coursing through my veins. I wasn't alone in this; my friends, my family, and even my customers were all in this together. After the meeting, Jenna sidled up beside me, her eyes sparkling with pride. "You were incredible, Maya! Seriously, you had him on the ropes. I almost expected him to sweat."

"Let's hope I didn't just provoke a tiger," I replied, the remnants of adrenaline buzzing in my system. "He's not one to back down easily."

"Neither are you," she countered, a playful nudge against my shoulder. "And besides, it's about time someone took a stand against the corporate machine. We need to gather more supporters. Tomorrow,

I'll help you bake a mountain of pastries. We'll take them around town, maybe even host a little 'Save the Bakery' event."

The idea sent a rush of warmth through me. I could already picture the familiar faces of my loyal customers lining up outside the bakery, ready to lend their support. "That sounds perfect! I can set up a petition too. Maybe we can get some media coverage."

"Now you're thinking like a true fighter!" she cheered, her enthusiasm contagious.

The following days were a whirlwind of flour, sugar, and community spirit. We transformed the bakery into a hub of activity, inviting customers to sign petitions and share their fondest memories. The air buzzed with laughter and the scent of baked goods, and for a moment, I allowed myself to believe we could win this battle.

But Mason was not a man easily deterred. I spotted him one afternoon, surveying the bakery from a distance, his expression inscrutable. My heart raced as I noticed how he seemed to absorb the atmosphere—the laughter, the camaraderie, the love that infused every corner of the shop. It was as if he were dissecting a complex puzzle, trying to decipher the heart of what made our bakery special.

"Hey, Earth to Maya!" Jenna's voice pulled me from my thoughts, her brow furrowed in concern. "You look like you've seen a ghost. What's going on?"

I shook my head, forcing a smile. "Just wondering what he's planning next. I can't shake the feeling that he's not done with us yet."

"Let him plot," she said dismissively, grabbing a tray of pastries. "We're building an army here. He can't take away something that means so much to so many people. Right?"

"You're right," I affirmed, but doubt lingered in my mind. The reality was, Mason Steele was a storm I couldn't ignore, a force of nature that could sweep through and erase everything I held dear.

As the days turned into a week, the community rallied. We collected signatures and shared stories that echoed through the streets, transforming into a tide of support. But just as I began to feel invincible, that familiar shadow loomed again.

The night before the city council's final vote, a storm raged outside, the wind howling like an angry beast. I sat alone in the bakery, the gentle glow of the overhead lights casting long shadows across the countertops. The sound of raindrops tapping against the windows provided a soothing backdrop to my racing thoughts.

My phone buzzed, pulling me from my musings. A text from Jenna read: Got some big news. Meet me at the café around the corner. It's important. My stomach churned with unease. I quickly grabbed my jacket and rushed out into the storm, rain pelting down like a thousand tiny fists.

When I arrived, Jenna was already there, her expression serious. "You need to see this." She held out her phone, the screen illuminating her worried face.

The headline read: Mason Steele's Company Announces Major Expansion Plans—Will Reshape Downtown.

"No," I breathed, the weight of the news crashing over me like a wave. "This can't be happening."

"Look at the bottom," Jenna urged, her finger tapping the screen. I squinted at the text, my heart sinking further. Steele plans to acquire local businesses for redevelopment, including Steele's Bakery, renowned for its community roots.

"Why would he target us directly?" I whispered, dread pooling in my stomach. "This isn't just a business deal for him; it's personal."

Jenna's eyes widened, understanding dawning on her. "He knows how much it means to you. He's trying to intimidate you before the vote."

Rage flared within me, mixing with despair. "I won't let him win. Not now, not ever."

Before Jenna could respond, my phone buzzed again, this time with an email notification. I opened it, my breath catching as I read the message. It was from Mason himself—a sleek, formal invitation to meet him the next day, just hours before the council vote.

"Are you going to go?" Jenna asked, her voice barely above a whisper.

"I have to," I replied, my voice steady but my heart racing with uncertainty. "If this is going to come to a head, I need to face him. But I won't walk into that meeting without a plan."

"Just promise me you won't do anything reckless," she cautioned, a hint of fear in her eyes.

"Reckless? Me?" I grinned wryly, but the weight of the situation pressed heavily on my chest. "I'll be careful. I just need to know what his endgame is."

As the storm raged outside, a different kind of tempest brewed within me—determination, defiance, and a fierce will to protect my family's legacy. I would face Mason Steele head-on, armed with my heart and the unwavering support of my community. But as I prepared for the confrontation ahead, a chilling thought crossed my mind: what if he had a card up his sleeve that could shatter everything I had fought for? The sense of impending danger loomed like thunderclouds overhead, waiting to burst.

Chapter 2: A Clash of Wills

The moment I stepped into Mason's office, the air thickened with unspoken tension. The expansive glass walls surrounding us felt more like a cage than a window to the bustling city beyond. I could hear the distant hum of life outside—cars honking, people laughing, and the occasional street musician attempting to woo passersby with a hopeful tune. But within those sleek walls, it was as if we existed in a bubble of hostility, poised for battle. Mason, with his tailored suit and razor-sharp jawline, sat like a king atop a throne, and I, armed only with my passion for literature and a determination that ran deeper than the roots of the ancient oak tree outside my bookstore, was prepared to fight for my territory.

"Your little bookstore is charming, but it's a relic of a bygone era," he declared, leaning back in his chair, fingers steepled like he was about to deliver a sermon. His tone dripped with condescension, and I felt my blood boil. "The world is moving forward, and frankly, it has no time for dusty shelves and quaint narratives."

"Dusty shelves?" I echoed, incredulous. "Those 'dusty shelves' hold the dreams of countless readers. You may see a relic, but I see a sanctuary—a place where stories come alive and hearts connect. It's not just a store; it's a community." My voice, though steady, carried a hint of defiance that I hoped would shatter his carefully constructed facade.

His brow arched, and that smug smile twisted into something more menacing. "A community? You mean a gathering of people stuck in nostalgia, unwilling to embrace the future? How very romantic of you." He leaned forward, and I could almost see the gears turning in his mind, calculating his next move. "I'm offering you a chance to join the revolution, to adapt, to thrive in a digital world."

"By bulldozing my bookstore? That's your version of revolution?" I shot back, feeling the heat of indignation rise to my cheeks. The contrast between us was stark—his ambition was sharp and clinical, while mine was raw and passionate. It was like comparing a finely honed sword to a wildflower, and I wouldn't let him cut me down.

"You're a businesswoman," he replied, his voice a low rumble, smoothing over the tension like a blanket over a jagged rock. "Don't you want to think bigger? There's an entire world out there, waiting for you to grasp it."

"Sure, but at what cost?" I countered, feeling the thrill of challenge surge through me. "At the cost of my integrity? My identity? I refuse to sacrifice the heart of my bookstore just to fit into a mold that someone like you deems acceptable. I built this place from the ground up, and it's not going anywhere."

His expression darkened, but I could see a flicker of interest behind his icy demeanor. "You talk about integrity as if it's a shield, but shields can only protect you for so long. The world is changing, and you're clinging to a fading dream. You need to evolve, or you'll end up as just another footnote in the annals of history."

I leaned closer, my heart pounding in my chest, daring to tread into territory that felt perilous. "And you think bulldozing a beloved bookstore is the answer? People don't just want to consume—they want connection, nostalgia, and warmth. You might have the plans, but I have the heart."

Mason's eyes narrowed, and for a moment, it felt like we were suspended in time, two titans locked in a duel of wills. There was an unspoken challenge simmering between us, a dance of power and resistance that crackled in the air like electricity. I could see it in the way his jaw tightened and how he clenched his fists, as if he were fighting against an instinctual attraction that neither of us dared to acknowledge.

Just then, the door swung open, and a flustered intern burst in, her eyes wide as if she'd stumbled into a lion's den. "Uh, Mr. Morgan, there's a—"

"Not now," Mason snapped, his attention still riveted on me, as if the intern were merely a ghost in the room. I couldn't help but feel a rush of satisfaction. In this moment, I had him distracted. "You were saying?" he prompted, returning his focus to me, that predatory glint in his eye making my stomach flutter uneasily.

"Maybe you should take a closer look at what you're trying to erase. Maybe it's more valuable than you realize," I said, my voice steady despite the tremors of adrenaline coursing through me.

His lips twitched, amusement breaking through his carefully crafted veneer. "Is that your final word? A sentimental plea?"

"Sentiment is powerful. It shapes decisions, motivates people, and builds communities. Maybe you're just too focused on numbers and metrics to see the value of the human experience," I shot back, my resolve strengthening as I felt the walls of his fortress begin to crack.

He leaned back, a thoughtful expression crossing his face, and for a moment, I wondered if I'd managed to plant a seed of doubt in his mind. But I quickly squashed that notion. He was a formidable opponent, and I wouldn't underestimate him.

Mason ran a hand through his hair, his irritation mingling with reluctant intrigue. "You really believe that, don't you? That a bookstore can stand against the tide of progress? I admire your passion, even if I think it's misplaced."

"Then let's find common ground," I suggested, channeling every ounce of creativity I possessed into that moment. "What if we could work together? You may have your vision, but I have the heart. We could create something new without sacrificing the old."

He paused, the air thick with possibilities. "Interesting proposition," he said slowly, weighing my words as if they were precious gems. "But it would take a lot more than just words to convince me."

"I'm not afraid of hard work," I replied, my spirit ignited by the challenge. "And I promise you, I'm just as relentless as you are. So, what do you say? Are you willing to see how a bookstore can not only survive but thrive alongside your vision?"

Mason's gaze bore into mine, and for a fleeting second, I thought I saw the faintest flicker of respect in his eyes. But just as quickly, it vanished, replaced by that familiar calculating intensity. He straightened, masking whatever emotion he might have been feeling beneath a layer of corporate coolness.

"Let's see what you've got," he said finally, his voice a low murmur that sent a shiver down my spine. "But don't think for a moment that I'll make this easy for you."

The gauntlet was thrown, and with it came the unspoken understanding that our battle was far from over. The clash of wills was only just beginning, and in that moment, amidst the icy disdain and simmering tension, I felt a pulse of something electric. This man was my adversary, but perhaps, just perhaps, he could also become my ally in an unexpected journey—one that neither of us had anticipated.

The days that followed our confrontation were steeped in a peculiar brew of defiance and resolve. Each morning, I would walk into my bookstore, a modest but vibrant space adorned with warm wooden shelves, inviting nooks, and a scent of aged paper that clung to the air like a beloved memory. It was my sanctuary, yet the weight of Mason's presence loomed larger than the stacks of novels that lined my walls. My mind raced with the implications of our exchange, replaying our heated discussion like a gripping novel I couldn't put down. The prospect of his relentless ambition and corporate vision felt like a storm gathering on the horizon.

As the sun dipped below the skyline, casting long shadows across the sidewalk, I set out to meet my best friend, Mia, for our weekly coffee ritual at a quaint café just a block away. The little place, adorned with fairy lights and an eclectic mix of mismatched furniture, was a favorite refuge for locals seeking respite from the city's chaos. When I pushed open the door, the warm, sweet aroma of freshly brewed coffee wrapped around me like a comforting hug.

Mia was already at our usual table, her dark curls bouncing as she animatedly recounted her latest dating disaster. "So, there I was, sitting at a fancy restaurant, dressed to the nines, and he shows up in sweatpants! Can you believe it?" She rolled her eyes dramatically, and I couldn't help but laugh.

"You have a knack for attracting the most interesting characters," I teased, sliding into the seat across from her. "I don't know whether to commend your taste in men or question your sanity."

"Both, probably," she quipped, taking a sip of her latte. "But enough about my love life. What's going on with you? Still sparring with the corporate gladiator?"

"More like fencing with a rhinoceros," I sighed, pouring out the details of my clash with Mason. With each word, the tension that had wrapped around my chest began to dissipate. "He's relentless, Mia. He thinks he can just steamroll over everything I've built."

"Can he?" she asked, leaning forward with a glimmer of mischief in her eyes. "I mean, is he right about the future? Are you really willing to let your bookstore slip into the past?"

The question hung in the air, a challenge I wasn't prepared for. "It's not about the future, it's about preserving the heart of what we do. People crave connection, stories that touch their souls. Mason sees numbers and graphs; I see lives intertwined through the pages of a book."

Mia nodded, her expression thoughtful. "So, you're saying you want to keep the soul of your bookstore alive, even if it means clashing with Mr. Steel Balls? Good luck with that."

"Steel Balls?" I burst out laughing, the tension of the day dissolving into mirth. "Is that your new nickname for him? I love it."

"Hey, if he can treat you like a pawn on his chessboard, I can certainly name him." She grinned, then shifted gears. "But really, have you thought about how you can fight back? It sounds like he's ready to bring the big guns, and I don't want to see you go down without a fight."

A glimmer of inspiration struck me then. "What if I host a community event? A weekend book fair, with local authors, live readings, and workshops. Something to remind people why they love books and the magic they create. Maybe even showcase how my bookstore is still relevant."

Mia's eyes sparkled with excitement. "That's brilliant! It'll not only draw people in but also demonstrate the bookstore's value to the community. If Mason thinks he can just obliterate you, he'll have to reckon with a whole bunch of book lovers ready to stand their ground."

I could feel the adrenaline surging through my veins as I envisioned the event unfolding—the chatter of excited patrons, the aroma of coffee mingling with pastries, the laughter of children captivated by storytelling sessions. But a thought pulled me back to reality. "What if he sabotages it? He has the resources and the connections. I'll be fighting a battle against his empire."

"Then make it a rallying cry," Mia said, leaning back with a triumphant smile. "A chance for the community to rally behind you. You know what they say—when you're fighting the dragon, you best gather the townsfolk to bring their pitchforks. You've got this."

Her enthusiasm was infectious, and I could feel the seed of determination taking root in my heart. "You're right. If I'm going to do this, I need to harness that energy and invite the very community Mason thinks he can erase. He'll see what we're made of."

As we sipped our drinks, the weight of my worries began to lift, replaced by the vibrant vision of the event. I could already imagine the banners fluttering in the breeze, the sound of laughter, and the joy of shared stories. Mason might have his vision of progress, but I had something more potent: a love for literature and a community that thrived on connection.

Just as I was getting lost in the possibilities, my phone buzzed with a text from an unknown number. Curiosity prickled at me as I pulled it out, a small knot forming in my stomach. The message read, "I heard about your bookstore and want to help. Meet me tomorrow at the usual spot."

The usual spot? A chill danced down my spine. Was it someone from the community or someone on Mason's radar? I quickly glanced at Mia, whose eyes were now wide with intrigue. "What does it say?"

"It's an invitation to meet someone who wants to help," I replied, my heart racing. "But I don't know who it is. It could be a trap."

"Or it could be your secret weapon," she countered, leaning forward, excitement bubbling over. "You're building an army, remember? Maybe this is just the reinforcement you need."

Despite my trepidation, I felt the spark of curiosity ignite within me. What if this was my chance to gain insight or allies? "Okay, I'll go," I said, the words tumbling out before I could second-guess myself. "But I'll be cautious."

Mia grinned, her eyes twinkling with mischief. "Just don't wear sweatpants."

We both laughed, the tension of the day ebbing away like the last remnants of twilight. In that moment, I realized that the battle with Mason was only just beginning, but I was ready to rally the troops. And perhaps, in doing so, I might just discover more than I bargained for—like allies, unexpected connections, and perhaps a little something that could turn this story into my own personal fairy tale.

I spent the night tossing and turning, the mystery of the text gnawing at me like an unfinished sentence. The café buzzed in my mind, the laughter and chatter echoing, merging with my own thoughts about the upcoming meeting. It felt like stepping into a story half-written, where I was both the protagonist and the author, wrestling with the twists and turns that could redefine my fate.

The next morning arrived with an uncharacteristically vibrant sun spilling through my window, illuminating the small room where I crafted dreams into words. As I prepared for the day, the anticipation of the unknown gripped me, transforming the mundane task of selecting an outfit into a battle of its own. I finally settled on a soft cream sweater and jeans, the fabric embracing me like a favorite book, comfortable yet versatile for whatever lay ahead.

When I reached the designated meeting place—an old-fashioned diner with a neon sign that flickered like a vintage postcard—the familiar scent of freshly brewed coffee and bacon wafted through the air. I stepped inside, the bell above the door chiming a friendly welcome. The warmth enveloped me, contrasting sharply with the cool air outside, and I spotted a booth in the back, its red vinyl cushions slightly worn but inviting.

Settling into the booth, I ordered a coffee, trying to quell the fluttering in my stomach. I scanned the room, my gaze darting from the bustling waitstaff to the patrons absorbed in their meals. With every tick of the clock, my mind spun with questions. Who would show up? A hopeful supporter? A double agent sent by Mason?

As I waited, I allowed my thoughts to wander, contemplating the book fair I planned to host. Would the community rally behind me? I imagined the faces of familiar customers—Mrs. Patterson, with her endless enthusiasm for historical romances, and the teenagers who would drop by after school, sharing snippets of their latest reads. If this meeting could help me garner support, it would be worth every nerve-wracking second.

Then, just as the clock struck ten, the door swung open, and a figure stepped inside. It was a woman, striking and confident, with bright red hair cascading over her shoulders like a fiery waterfall. Her green coat stood out like a beacon against the muted tones of the diner, and she scanned the room with a purposeful gaze before striding toward me.

"Are you the one who sent for help?" she asked, her voice sharp and full of energy, as she slid into the seat across from me.

"I... I received a text," I replied, still trying to absorb her presence. "You're the one?"

"Call me Clara," she said, leaning forward. "I heard about your bookstore and the battle you're facing against that corporate shark. Mason Morgan, right?"

I nodded, feeling an unexpected surge of relief wash over me. "Yes, exactly. He thinks he can take over without a second thought."

"Not if I have anything to say about it." Clara's eyes sparkled with determination, and I could feel the energy radiating off her. "I've been a part of the community for years, and I know a lot of people who love that bookstore. It's an institution!"

"Really?" My heart leaped at the thought of potential allies. "What do you propose?"

"I've organized events like the one you're planning before. We can host a literary festival—make it bigger than just a book fair. If we bring in local authors, food trucks, and music, we can turn this into a block party! A celebration of all things books." She beamed, her excitement infectious.

"That sounds incredible!" I replied, my thoughts racing as I envisioned the possibilities. "But how do we get the word out? Mason's got the marketing muscle."

Clara waved her hand dismissively. "Let me worry about that. I've got connections. We'll use social media, community boards, and good old-fashioned word of mouth. And once people start to see what we're doing, they'll flock to it. The key is to create a buzz, and I have some ideas on how to do that."

As she spoke, I could feel the vision of our festival blossoming in my mind. The scent of coffee and breakfast filled the air, but the richness of her words was more intoxicating than any brew. "You seem to know a lot about organizing these events. Have you done this before?"

"Once or twice," she said, a hint of modesty in her tone. "I've helped with charity events and community gatherings. But this—this is personal for me. I grew up around here, and I want to see our culture preserved, not erased."

Before I could respond, the door swung open again, and in walked Mason. The world seemed to freeze for a heartbeat. He strode in with the same undeniable confidence, dressed in a crisp, dark suit that made him look like he was heading to a boardroom meeting. His gaze immediately locked onto mine, and I felt my heart skip a beat, adrenaline coursing through my veins.

"Of all the diners in the city, you had to choose this one?" he remarked, his voice smooth yet edged with annoyance. "I didn't think you'd be here, playing the damsel in distress."

"Is that what you think?" I shot back, unwilling to back down even in the face of his formidable presence. "I'm actually in the middle of a strategy meeting."

"Is that what you call it?" He glanced at Clara, his eyes narrowing. "And who's your friend? Another dreamer hoping to save a dying industry?"

Clara's composure was remarkable, and she shot back with a fierce smile, "Actually, I'm here to help this bookstore thrive. Something your corporation clearly doesn't understand."

Mason smirked, clearly amused by the boldness of my newfound ally. "Good luck with that. You'll need it."

I felt the tension escalate, a storm brewing in the small space, but I refused to show any sign of intimidation. "You underestimate us, Mason. You think this is just about a bookstore? This is about a community. And we're not going anywhere."

The smirk faded from his lips, replaced by a look of genuine surprise. For the first time, I saw a flicker of uncertainty in his eyes, as if my words had pricked at the edge of his armor. But just as quickly, he masked it, slipping back into his composed facade.

"Enjoy your little meeting, ladies," he said, the sardonic edge returning to his voice as he turned to leave. "But remember, the clock is ticking. Change is coming, whether you like it or not."

As the door closed behind him, a silence enveloped us, thick with tension. Clara and I exchanged glances, the weight of his words hanging in the air like an uninvited guest.

"What do you think he meant by that?" I asked, feeling a knot of apprehension tighten in my stomach.

"Who knows with him?" Clara replied, her brow furrowed. "But we have to keep moving forward. If he's that threatened, it means we're on the right track."

I nodded, the fire in my gut rekindling. This was not just a battle for my bookstore; it was a stand against a corporate titan who thought he could crush dreams beneath the heel of his polished shoes.

But as we began to outline our plans for the festival, my phone buzzed again, interrupting our momentum. Glancing at the screen, my heart plummeted.

It was a message from Mason.

"Don't say I didn't warn you. You have no idea what you're up against."

A chill shot down my spine, and I looked at Clara, her expression mirroring my own growing dread.

"What does he mean?" I whispered, my heart racing.

In that moment, I knew that the battle ahead was going to be far more dangerous than I'd ever anticipated, and Mason Morgan was a formidable adversary, one who wouldn't back down without a fight. And as the clock ticked on, I realized that time was not on our side.

Chapter 3: The Terms

The air in the room felt thick, electric with tension as Mason leaned against the wall, arms crossed, a smirk playing at the corners of his lips. The golden light filtering through the window caught the sharp angles of his jaw, making him look more like a predator than a man negotiating over the ruins of my father's legacy. My heart thudded painfully in my chest, a wild rhythm that echoed my growing unease.

"Are you done?" he asked, tilting his head, the arrogance in his tone wrapping around his words like silk. "Because I'm just getting started."

His confidence was a weapon, one I had seen too many times in the business world. I straightened my back, refusing to let him see how rattled I felt. "This isn't a game for me, Mason," I shot back, my voice steady even as my mind raced to find a way out of this tangled web he was spinning. "This is my father's dream, not some corporate takeover you can shove down my throat."

He chuckled, a low, rich sound that filled the space between us with a disarming warmth, as if I had made a joke instead of declaring war. "Your father's dream?" His eyes flickered with something—challenge, perhaps? "What a quaint notion. But let's be honest here. Dreams don't pay the bills. I'm offering you a way to turn that dream into a thriving business."

Each word fell like stones into a pond, sending ripples of doubt through my resolve. But I couldn't let him see that. "A thriving business that belongs to you, not to us," I replied, forcing myself to meet his gaze. "You think I'd sell my father's dream to the highest bidder just to line your pockets?"

Mason pushed off the wall and stepped closer, the scent of his cologne enveloping me, mingling with the floral notes of the garden just outside the window. It was distracting and dangerously intoxicating. "Look around," he gestured with a sweeping hand, indicating the modest office filled with faded pictures of my father at various milestones. "This place is a museum. I can turn it into something great. You just have to give me the chance."

I glanced around, feeling the weight of nostalgia mixed with a fierce protectiveness. This wasn't just an office; it was a shrine to my father's passion, a canvas of his dreams splattered with sweat and hard work. "You don't get it, do you? This isn't just a business deal for me. This is family. It's everything I've ever known."

His expression shifted, a flicker of something softer—sympathy? Regret? But it vanished as quickly as it appeared, replaced by that signature steeliness that I had come to loathe. "You think holding on to this place will somehow keep your father alive? He's gone, and clinging to memories won't bring him back."

The jab hit harder than I expected, stirring a whirlwind of emotions I thought I had locked away. "You don't know anything about me or my father," I said, voice trembling slightly. "He believed in this place, and I won't let you turn it into a soulless corporation. You're just like everyone else, wanting to take and take without understanding what this really means."

"Maybe you need to open your eyes, then." Mason's voice dropped to a low murmur, almost conspiratorial. "If you want to keep his legacy alive, you have to let go of the past and adapt to the future."

I shook my head, my anger flaring like a flame. "This isn't about adaptation; it's about respect. My father built this from the ground up. He poured his heart into it, and you want to bulldoze it for profit. You're the one who needs to change, Mason."

For a moment, we stood in silence, the air thick with our unspoken words, a duel of wills locked in an unyielding embrace. I felt the heat radiating from him, a magnetic force that both repelled and drew me in. How infuriating that he could make me feel so vulnerable yet so defiant at the same time.

His expression softened for just a heartbeat, and I dared to hope for a crack in his armor. "Look," he said, voice low and steady, "what if we made a deal? You get your say, and I'll incorporate your ideas. This can be a partnership."

"Partnership?" I repeated, disbelief coloring my tone. "You mean like you telling me how things are going to work while I sit in the corner with a smile and a wave?"

"No, I'm offering you a chance to have a voice," he countered, stepping closer, invading my space with a confidence that was both infuriating and oddly appealing. "To shape this into something that honors your father while still making it profitable."

A dangerous idea flickered in my mind, the image of a joint venture twisting and turning in a thousand different ways, each more tempting than the last. But beneath that temptation lay a deeper fear, one I couldn't shake off. "And what's in it for you? You don't strike me as someone who does anything without a personal agenda."

His smile returned, sharper than before, revealing a glimpse of the man hidden beneath the layers of arrogance. "You're right, I don't do anything without a reason. But I'll let you in on a secret: I have my reasons for wanting this to succeed. And, believe it or not, it goes beyond profit."

I didn't know whether to laugh or scoff at his bold claim. The man was a walking contradiction, capable of charming a room while simultaneously exuding a coldness that made my skin crawl. "So, what's your angle? Trying to play the knight in shining armor?"

"More like the investor who recognizes potential when he sees it," he replied smoothly. "I don't expect you to trust me right away, but I can help you preserve what you value most."

I wanted to laugh. What a gallant notion for a man who thrived in a world of cutthroat deals and relentless ambition. But there was a part of me, buried deep beneath the surface, that craved the chance to breathe new life into my father's dream without losing its essence. The idea of collaboration loomed enticingly, but I knew the danger of getting too close to someone like Mason.

"Trust isn't given; it's earned," I said firmly, hoping to sound more resolute than I felt. "So, if we're going to talk terms, let's do it on equal footing."

He raised an eyebrow, intrigued, and for a fleeting moment, I thought I saw the glimmer of respect in his gaze. "Equal footing? That's a tall order, but I'm willing to entertain it."

And just like that, the game shifted, the stakes rising higher than ever before, the ground beneath us quaking with potential—both exhilarating and terrifying in equal measure.

The sun dipped lower in the sky, casting long shadows across the room as Mason's words lingered in the air. They felt like a chain, each syllable a heavy link binding me to a future I hadn't chosen. My fingers tightened around the edge of the desk, a sturdy lifeline in the storm brewing between us. Mason's presence loomed like a storm cloud, dark and electric, filled with potential for either destruction or renewal.

"Let's be real," he continued, voice smooth as silk yet edged with steel. "This isn't just about you. It's about survival. The market is ruthless, and your father's dream—while beautiful—needs a solid foundation if it's going to thrive."

I wanted to throw something at him. Perhaps the paperweight shaped like a globe that represented everything my father had stood for—a world built on dreams and integrity. "Survival doesn't mean selling your soul," I shot back, wishing my voice didn't tremble with the weight of my conviction. "This isn't just some investment opportunity for you; it's my life's work."

Mason raised an eyebrow, a flicker of interest sparking in his gaze. "Life's work, you say? Yet here you are, sitting in a room that looks like a time capsule from the '90s. You've been living in the shadow of your father's legacy instead of forging your own path."

The sharpness of his critique pierced through the air, leaving a raw ache in its wake. My father's dream had been more than just a business; it had been a beacon of hope and community, a place where people felt seen and valued. I couldn't let Mason reduce it to mere numbers on a spreadsheet. "You think you know me, but you don't," I snapped, the anger bubbling to the surface like hot lava. "I'm not some helpless heiress waiting for a prince to come rescue me from the past."

"Helpless? Oh no," he replied, stepping closer, a glint of amusement in his eyes. "You're like a lion backed into a corner, all claws and teeth. But tell me, how effective are those claws if you don't know how to use them?"

"Enough!" I spat, refusing to let him rattle me further. "If you want to negotiate, then let's do it. But this is not a battle of wills; it's a matter of principles."

"Principles," he echoed, the word rolling off his tongue with a mocking lilt. "What are principles worth in this day and age? They don't pay the rent, and they certainly don't pay for the renovations this place so desperately needs."

I fought to keep my breath steady, my thoughts racing. He was right about one thing: this place needed a revival. But not the kind he was offering, slick and soulless. "And you think bulldozing everything in sight is the answer?" I shot back, feeling the tide of desperation rise in me. "You can't strip away the heart and expect it to beat."

Mason paused, his expression softening again, but only for a moment. "Heart is all well and good until it's trampled underfoot by competition. You need to adapt or die. Isn't that what you learned in business school?"

"I learned that people are what make a business thrive," I retorted, feeling the heat of the conversation boil over into something tangible, something electric. "You might understand numbers, but I understand people. There's a reason my father's legacy means so much to this community. He connected with them."

Mason nodded, his gaze piercing. "Then help me connect with them. We can transform this into a community hub—one that still honors your father's vision, but with a fresh spin. Let's make it something they'll rally around."

"Rally around?" I laughed, incredulous. "You mean your corporate spin on nostalgia? That's rich."

"Not nostalgia," he corrected smoothly, stepping even closer. "A revival. There's a difference. And you know it. The world is changing, and people are hungry for authenticity. We can be that beacon—together."

For a brief moment, the idea hung between us, tantalizing and treacherous. The thought of breathing new life into this place was intoxicating. But could I trust him?

"I'm not asking for a partnership in name only, Mason. I want a say in how this place evolves," I insisted, looking straight into his eyes. "If I'm going to put my father's legacy on the line, it better be worth it."

A smile broke across his face, a genuine one that took me off guard. "Now that's a negotiation I can work with. I don't want just a piece of the pie; I want you to help me bake it. You have the vision, and I have the resources."

The way he spoke was as if we were crafting something grand, a work of art rather than a mere business deal. But beneath the surface, I could sense a catch, something lurking in the shadows. "And what's the price, Mason?"

"Let's just say I want more than just your agreement. I want your passion, your commitment. You can't half-ass this if you expect me to invest."

"That's a tall order," I said, crossing my arms, feeling the tension between us shift like the very air we breathed. "And how do I know you won't just walk away if things get tough?"

"Because I'm not just some suit looking to flip a property for a quick profit. I'm in this for the long haul," he replied, sincerity spilling from his lips, though doubt still lurked in the corners of my mind.

"Words, Mason. I've heard enough of those."

"Then let's turn those words into action. We'll draft an agreement together, outlining everything. You'll see I'm a man of my word."

I weighed his offer carefully, the idea of partnership pulling at me like an undercurrent. If I was going to make this work, I had to set aside my skepticism, at least for a moment. "Alright, let's talk specifics then. But know this: I will fight for my father's vision every step of the way."

His smile returned, wider this time, as if I had just handed him the keys to a treasure chest. "Then let's get to work, shall we?"

But just as I turned to gather my thoughts, the door swung open. My assistant, Emma, entered with a flurry of papers in hand, her face a mask of concern. "Sorry to interrupt, but I thought you'd want to know—"

"What is it?" I asked, anxiety creeping back in as I glanced at Mason, who looked equally curious.

"There's been a bit of a situation at the community center," Emma said, her voice dropping to a whisper. "Some protesters are demanding to speak with you. They heard about the potential changes."

Mason's expression hardened, and for a fleeting moment, I caught a glimpse of vulnerability behind his confident facade. "Protests?" he repeated, the weight of reality crashing back in around us.

"Yes, it seems they're worried about losing their gathering space." Emma's eyes darted between us, sensing the tension brewing.

I exchanged a quick look with Mason, the unspoken understanding that we both had more at stake than we realized. The idea of partnering to create something meaningful now felt more urgent than ever, but the path ahead was fraught with obstacles.

"Let's go," I said, determination rising within me like a phoenix from the ashes. "We'll face them together."

Mason nodded, the flicker of respect igniting once more. We both stepped forward, ready to confront the challenges ahead—two unlikely allies drawn together by a shared vision, despite the shadows of doubt still lingering between us.

Emma's voice snapped me back into the present, grounding me as the weight of her news hung like an anvil in the air. The protesters gathered at the community center were no mere inconvenience; they were a stark reminder of the battle I was stepping into, one that required more than just courage and clever words. It needed the kind of finesse I had yet to acquire.

"We need to act quickly," I said, glancing at Mason, who now looked less like a corporate marauder and more like a man suddenly aware of the repercussions of his ambitions. "If they're already here, it means they're serious about this."

"Good," he replied, adjusting the cuffs of his shirt with an air of confidence that bordered on arrogance. "Let's give them something to talk about. We'll turn this around to our advantage."

"Are you always this dismissive?" I shot back, crossing my arms in defiance. "These are people's lives we're talking about. Their community, their home."

"Precisely," he countered, meeting my gaze with unyielding intensity. "And if we're going to make this work, we need to win their support, not just their tolerance."

With that, he strode toward the door, exuding an almost palpable charisma that was both infuriating and intoxicating. I trailed behind him, my mind racing through a list of possible scenarios. What would I say? How would I address the fears and frustrations of those who had every right to feel threatened? The weight of the past pressed heavily on my shoulders, yet I couldn't shake the feeling that this was the pivotal moment for the future of my father's legacy.

As we stepped outside, the sounds of a growing crowd washed over us. Murmurs swirled like autumn leaves caught in a breeze, turning into shouts that pierced through the air. I could see their faces, a mix of determination and fear, a collective heartbeat resonating with a single pulse: protect what we have.

"Mason, you're in charge of the crowd. I'll handle the messaging," I instructed, trying to mask the apprehension in my voice.

"Fine by me," he replied, brushing off my directive with a casual wave of his hand. "Just remember, the louder the roar, the greater the opportunity."

Before I could respond, he stepped forward, calling out to the assembled crowd, his voice smooth and commanding. "Ladies and gentlemen! Thank you for gathering here today! We understand your concerns and are here to listen."

The crowd surged forward, fueled by passion, and I felt a rush of adrenaline. It was time to step up, to reclaim my voice. "Mason, wait!" I whispered, suddenly uncertain about the man I had been compelled to partner with.

But he didn't stop. "I believe in change," he continued, his tone deliberate. "I believe in progress. And I believe we can work together to make this community even stronger."

"Stronger?" a woman shouted from the front, her face flushed with emotion. "Stronger how? By tearing down what we've built?"

"By building something better!" Mason declared, a glimmer of that fierce ambition shining in his eyes. "Imagine a space where we can host events, workshops, and gatherings that reflect the vibrant life of this community!"

The crowd simmered, caught between his words and their fears. I could see a glimmer of hope flickering in some of their eyes, but the doubts were just as palpable.

I stepped forward, my heart pounding, ready to bridge the chasm that Mason's words had opened. "We're here to listen," I said, my voice steady as I locked eyes with the woman who had spoken up. "Tell us what you need, what you value. We want to ensure this space continues to serve you, not just our business."

Mason shot me a look of surprise, as if he hadn't expected me to step in like this. "Exactly," he chimed in, recovering quickly. "Your voices matter. We need your feedback to create something that reflects our shared vision."

The woman stepped forward, fists clenched at her sides. "You don't understand. This isn't just about renovations; this is our home. We've hosted events here for decades. We can't let it turn into a glossy façade for tourists or—"

"Or another soulless venture," I finished for her, feeling a surge of solidarity. "You have every right to be worried. But I promise you, I will fight to keep this place alive in a way that honors its history and all of you."

Mason nodded, sensing the shift in momentum. "Together, we can revitalize it while preserving its heart," he added, his gaze moving over the crowd, urging them to see the potential for collaboration.

The woman regarded us skeptically, glancing around at the faces of her neighbors. "How do we know you won't just take what you want and leave us with nothing?"

"We don't expect anything from you except honesty," I said, trying to ground the conversation. "Help us understand your vision, and we'll work together to make it happen."

Slowly, the atmosphere began to shift, a crack forming in the wall of suspicion that surrounded us. "Alright," she said, arms crossed but her voice softer. "We want to keep this community space. We want our events and gatherings. Can you promise us that?"

"I can promise you that we will protect it," I replied, sincerity lacing my tone. "This isn't just about business for me; it's personal. My father believed in this place, and I do too."

Mason's gaze darted to me, surprise mingling with admiration. I could feel the crackle of energy between us, the weight of potential lingering in the air. "And together, we can ensure it thrives," he added, his voice lower, as if he too felt the gravity of the moment.

A murmured agreement rippled through the crowd, tentative but real. Then, just as we seemed to be finding common ground, a voice rose above the rest, piercing the hopeful atmosphere like a knife. "But what about the plans? We've seen blueprints, and they don't include any of our needs."

The woman's face paled, and I felt a rush of dread wash over me. "What plans?" I asked, my stomach dropping.

A man stepped forward, shaking his head. "The plans were sent to the council. They're trying to push them through without public input."

Mason's expression darkened, his posture shifting as he sensed the tension rising again. "Plans? I wasn't aware of any finalized blueprints," he said, his voice clipped, the charming veneer cracking.

"I knew it," I breathed, realization dawning like an unwelcome light. "They're trying to bypass us entirely."

Mason's eyes narrowed, his earlier bravado vanishing. "This wasn't part of our deal. If they're moving forward without us, we need to stop them. Now."

Panic surged through me, igniting a fire of determination. "We can't let this happen. If we don't act fast, we risk losing everything."

But before I could formulate a plan, a sharp voice cut through the growing noise, one that froze me in my tracks. "You want to save this place, do you? Then you better be ready for a fight."

I turned to see the city planner, a formidable woman with a reputation for being merciless. "Because I assure you, I won't let sentimentality get in the way of progress."

Mason shifted beside me, the tension between us thickening as we both realized the battle lines were being drawn. "What do you mean?" he asked, the confidence in his voice wavering slightly.

She stepped closer, a predatory gleam in her eyes. "I mean, if you want to stop the renovations, you're going to have to prove your worth. I'm not interested in nostalgia."

With every word, the stakes soared higher, and I could feel the weight of the crowd's hopes and fears bearing down on us. This was no longer a simple negotiation; it was war, and the outcome would define everything I had fought to protect.

"Then let's show her what we're made of," I said, locking eyes with Mason, our shared resolve igniting an unexpected spark between us.

But just as we prepared to confront the city planner, a loud crash echoed through the crowd, causing everyone to turn. My heart raced as I glimpsed the commotion, a sea of bodies shifting as chaos erupted.

"Get back!" someone shouted, panic spreading like wildfire.

I barely had time to process what was happening before the world around me spiraled into chaos, the ground shifting beneath my feet as I braced myself for the storm to come.

Chapter 4: Tensions Rise

The air in the office crackled with tension, electric and unnerving, as I squared my shoulders and marched into Mason's domain. He sat behind a massive oak desk, papers strewn like fallen leaves in autumn, the light catching his tousled hair and the sharp angles of his jaw. Everything about him radiated a careless confidence that grated on my nerves, yet a tiny part of me—a part I loathed—found it oddly captivating. With every encounter, I felt like a moth drawn to his flame, perilous and utterly foolish.

"Do you ever stop to think?" I snapped, slamming the contract down in front of him. The sound echoed, a sharp contrast to the otherwise hushed atmosphere. "We're in a time crunch, and you're too busy playing chess with these numbers to notice that we're losing the game!"

His gaze lifted, a slow, deliberate motion, and a smirk tugged at the corners of his lips. "Chess is a game of strategy, Avery. Something you might consider employing instead of throwing tantrums."

"Tantrums? You think this is a tantrum?" I leaned closer, my voice low but intense. "I'm trying to save this project from becoming a disaster of epic proportions. Maybe you could try prioritizing efficiency over ego for once."

He leaned back in his chair, folding his arms across his chest, eyes glinting with amusement. "And yet here you are, flailing about like a fish out of water. How charming."

Charm. The word hung in the air like an unsought perfume, pungent yet alluring, and I found my pulse quickening in response to his playful taunt. I straightened, indignation blooming within me like a vivid flower, bright and defiant. "This isn't a game, Mason! If we miss the deadline, it's not just our reputations on the line. We could lose the contract altogether!"

With a lazy flick of his wrist, he dismissed my concern. "If we're being honest, Avery, I have no intention of losing. The numbers will work in our favor; they always do."

I stared at him, incredulous. How could he be so infuriatingly confident, so thoroughly convinced of his own superiority? It was maddening. "You need to stop relying on luck and start recognizing the urgency of our situation."

"Urgency? Is that what you call it?" His tone shifted, playful to sardonic, a dance I was becoming far too accustomed to. "Perhaps you're just feeling the weight of your own expectations, rather than mine."

He struck a nerve. Expectations—his expectations—and the thought of disappointing him twisted something inside me. It wasn't just the project I feared failing; it was the idea of him seeing me as anything less than capable.

"Let's not pretend we're friends, Mason," I replied, forcing my voice to steady. "You see me as nothing more than a means to an end, and I'm tired of playing along."

"Ah, there it is." His eyes sparkled with something I couldn't quite place, an emotion that danced just beyond my reach. "The truth slips through the cracks when the pressure rises."

Before I could respond, the intercom buzzed with an announcement, breaking the simmering tension. "Avery, you have a call on line two."

I backed away from his desk, anger and confusion mingling in my chest as I reached for the phone. "I'll be right back," I muttered, not waiting for a response. I needed a moment to collect myself, to extinguish the embers of irritation that threatened to ignite into something much more dangerous.

The call was a client, one I had worked diligently to keep happy amidst the chaos Mason created. As I spoke, I felt the weight of his gaze, a tangible presence behind me, watching, assessing. It sent shivers skittering up my spine, not entirely unpleasant yet wholly distracting.

After hanging up, I turned back to find Mason leaning against the doorframe, arms crossed, his expression unreadable. "You handled that well," he said, the compliment unexpected and disarming.

"Don't get used to it," I shot back, heart racing. "You're still a nightmare to work with."

"Is that so?" His lips curled into a teasing smile, and I could feel the room closing in, the air thickening around us. "Perhaps I'm just pushing you to be better."

I scoffed, feigning indifference. "Or pushing me to the edge of insanity."

He stepped closer, the distance between us evaporating. "Which do you prefer? Insanity or mediocrity?"

I opened my mouth to retort, but the words faltered as I caught a glimmer of something genuine in his eyes. This wasn't just antagonism; there was an undercurrent of challenge, perhaps even camaraderie, that stirred something within me. A flicker of curiosity, a flicker I was determined to snuff out.

"I prefer neither," I finally managed, my voice low and steady. "I prefer working with someone who respects the urgency of our tasks."

His laughter, low and rich, reverberated in my chest, unsettling me further. "And yet here we are, both of us embroiled in this dance of defiance. Admit it, Avery; you love the challenge."

"Love it? Not quite," I replied, crossing my arms defiantly. "But I won't back down from it either. So let's find a way to navigate this without driving each other mad."

He tilted his head, a playful smirk still plastered on his face. "Madness seems to be your forte, after all."

I rolled my eyes, a small smile creeping in despite my resolve. "You really think so highly of yourself, don't you?"

"Only when it comes to matters of the heart," he replied, his voice dropping to a conspiratorial whisper. "And business, of course."

My heart raced, defiance clashing with the undeniable chemistry simmering in the air. Here we were, two adversaries caught in a web of ambition, attraction, and a mutual disdain that might just be hiding something deeper. Yet, I couldn't let myself delve into that territory; it was far too dangerous.

"I'm not going to play your games, Mason," I declared, turning to leave, though I could feel his eyes boring into me, that persistent curiosity tugging at my resolve.

"Games?" he called after me, voice low and teasing. "Oh, I assure you, Avery, this is just the beginning."

The next morning arrived with a heavy sky, gray clouds marching across the horizon like a battalion preparing for battle. I walked into the office feeling the weight of my own resolve—today would be different. Today, I wouldn't let Mason's sardonic charm get under my skin. I had my coffee in hand, the rich aroma swirling around me like a protective shield, but I knew it wouldn't be enough to deter the inevitable clash.

As I settled at my desk, the hum of the office enveloped me, punctuated by the sound of clicking keyboards and hushed conversations. Mason's office door stood ajar, and I could see him hunched over a set of documents, his brow furrowed in concentration. The sight did something peculiar to my stomach—a mix of irritation and an inexplicable urge to know what was occupying his mind.

"Coffee?" I asked, turning my head toward him, deciding to initiate an olive branch in our ongoing war of wills.

"Only if it's not burnt this time," he quipped, looking up from his papers. His eyes gleamed with that familiar spark, and I fought the urge to roll mine.

"Burnt coffee? That's rich coming from someone who considers reheating leftovers an art form." I couldn't resist the jab, a playful spark igniting in the air between us.

Mason raised an eyebrow, a bemused smile playing on his lips. "You'd be surprised by the depth of my culinary expertise. You might even call me a connoisseur of convenience."

"Connoisseur of convenience?" I laughed, unable to hold back. "Now that's a title I can get behind."

The moment hung between us, charged and peculiar. For a split second, the world outside faded, leaving just the two of us in our own ridiculous banter. It was an odd relief, a temporary ceasefire in our ongoing skirmish. But just as quickly, I pulled myself back, reminded that this was merely a diversion, a way to mask the discomfort simmering beneath the surface.

I returned to my desk, clutching my steaming cup, and tried to focus on the task at hand. But Mason's presence loomed, an invisible thread binding us together despite my best efforts to sever it. The day wore on, filled with calls and meetings that felt increasingly hollow without our usual sparring.

Later, as the afternoon sun struggled to pierce through the clouds, Mason breezed into my office, his stride confident and assured. "Avery, have you seen the latest projections?"

"Not yet. I was too busy dealing with the fallout from your last 'brilliant' idea," I shot back, hoping to maintain my composure. "You know, the one that almost derailed the project."

He chuckled, that maddeningly charming sound sending a thrill down my spine. "You do know that panic only intensifies the situation, don't you? If you'd relaxed just a bit, you might have noticed how close we are to meeting our goals."

"Relax? You're asking me to relax while you dance on the precipice of disaster? No thanks," I replied, rolling my eyes, even as my heart raced at the challenge in his gaze.

His smirk widened. "Admit it, Avery, you love the thrill of it. The uncertainty. It's practically your middle name."

"My middle name is actually Marie," I shot back, though I felt a grin tugging at my lips despite my best efforts to remain stoic. "And I have no interest in thrilling uncertainties, thank you very much."

"Sure you don't." Mason leaned against the doorframe, arms crossed, a picture of casual confidence. "But it's in those moments of chaos that you really shine, isn't it? All that passion of yours ignites, and I can't help but admire the fire."

I took a breath, searching for a clever retort, but his compliment, though veiled in playful sarcasm, lingered longer than intended. "Stop trying to flatter me, Mason. I'm not falling for your games."

"Games? Oh no, my dear Avery, this is no game. This is survival of the fittest." His gaze was unwavering, piercing through the layers of my defenses.

"Survival? I'd call it more like self-inflicted torture," I quipped, feeling a rush of adrenaline as I leaned back in my chair, folding my arms. "You're just one more missed deadline away from being declared a villain in my personal narrative."

"Every good story needs a villain," he replied, a mischievous glint in his eye. "Besides, I thought you enjoyed the complexity of characters."

"Complexity?" I echoed, raising an eyebrow. "Is that what you call it? I thought it was just your version of a bad attitude."

"Touché," he conceded, the smile fading momentarily. "But you'd be surprised how much lies beneath the surface, Avery. What you perceive as a bad attitude could very well be a desire for excellence. Not everyone sees the world in black and white."

"Or perhaps you're just too self-absorbed to recognize when you're crossing lines," I countered, my heart racing as the conversation turned more serious. "There's a difference between pushing for excellence and disregarding the team's efforts."

For a moment, silence enveloped us, and I felt the shift in the air. Mason's eyes narrowed, a flicker of something deeper passing between us—frustration, perhaps, or understanding. "You know, I respect your determination. It's refreshing in a world full of complacency."

"Respect? That's a new one." My voice softened, caught off guard by his sincerity. "I didn't think you had it in you."

"Don't mistake my confidence for arrogance, Avery. I recognize talent when I see it." His tone had shifted, more earnest now, and it set my heart fluttering. "You may not want to admit it, but we make a good team when we're not at each other's throats."

"I wouldn't go that far," I retorted, trying to mask the warmth creeping into my cheeks. "We're more like an odd couple—fire and ice."

"Then let's see what happens when fire meets ice." His words hung in the air, a challenge laced with something I couldn't quite place.

Before I could respond, my phone buzzed on the desk, pulling me back to reality. It was a message from one of our clients, asking for a meeting to discuss the project timeline. I sighed, the weight of responsibility crashing back over me. "I have to take this."

"Of course," he said, stepping aside, but the tension remained, a palpable force binding us even as I turned my attention back to work.

As I dealt with the client's demands, I couldn't shake the feeling that something had shifted between us. Mason's teasing façade had cracked, revealing glimpses of a man who was far more complex than I had first imagined. The realization unsettled me, tugging at threads of curiosity and annoyance that I had yet to unravel.

After wrapping up the call, I glanced back at him, only to find he was already watching me, an inscrutable expression on his face. "You know, Avery," he said, voice low, "sometimes it's not about winning or losing. It's about understanding the game and playing it your way."

My heart raced again, and I could only nod, feeling the walls I had built around myself beginning to waver. The battlefield of our relationship was no longer just about contracts and deadlines; it was evolving into something much more intricate, and I wasn't sure if I was ready for the complexities that lay ahead.

The sun dipped low on the horizon, casting long shadows that stretched like the tendrils of our ongoing feud. I sat at my desk, the faint hum of the office serving as a backdrop to the war waging within me. As the day wore on, my resolve to stay detached was tested repeatedly by Mason's relentless charm and that disarming smile that made it hard to remember why I was supposed to despise him.

As I rifled through the paperwork, my mind wandered to the meetings we'd had—every sharp word, every glimmer of amusement in his eyes. It was exhausting, battling him while also feeling like I was engaged in a dance that neither of us fully understood.

The door swung open with a dramatic flourish, and Mason strode in, a coffee cup in hand and a confident grin plastered on his face. "You know, if you spent less time glowering at your paperwork and more time enjoying your coffee, you might actually learn to appreciate its flavor," he said, leaning against my desk.

"Why would I appreciate a drink that tastes like burnt rubber?" I replied, keeping my tone as icy as I could manage. "Especially when I have to listen to your incessant rambling."

He feigned offense, a hand over his heart. "Rambling? I prefer to think of it as enlightening conversation. You should try it sometime."

"Enlightening? Please. Enlightenment is not what I seek when I'm buried under a mountain of work." I leaned back, crossing my arms defiantly, daring him to continue.

"Then let me help lighten your load," he offered, the sincerity in his voice surprising me. "We can tackle these projections together. Maybe we'll even find some common ground between your panic and my confidence."

"Common ground?" I echoed, incredulous. "You mean your constant need to take risks while I'm trying to stabilize this project? That's a delightful recipe for disaster."

"Stabilizing is all well and good, but you can't spell 'excitement' without 'x,'" he quipped, his grin widening.

"Oh yes, because excitement is precisely what we need when the deadline is creeping up like a shadow in a horror movie," I shot back, my frustration spilling over.

Mason stepped closer, lowering his voice conspiratorially. "Maybe you just need to embrace the chaos. You're too focused on the finish line, Avery. Life isn't always about being practical. Sometimes you need to take a leap and trust that you'll land on your feet."

"And sometimes that leap lands you flat on your face," I countered, my voice dropping to a whisper, the tension between us palpable.

"Ah, but isn't that the fun of it? To get back up, brush yourself off, and prove to the world that you're tougher than it gives you credit for?"

I blinked at him, taken aback by the earnestness in his gaze. "And what if I don't want to take that leap with you, Mason? What if I prefer my safe little bubble?"

"Then I suppose we'll be stuck in this bubble of tension, forever pushing each other's buttons." He leaned back slightly, the corners of his mouth still quirking upward. "And what a tragic loss that would be."

"You're impossible," I murmured, irritation and amusement colliding within me.

"I prefer 'incredibly charming,'" he replied, unfazed by my retort. "So, shall we dive into these projections together? If nothing else, you'll have an entertaining story to tell."

"Fine," I conceded, my voice tinged with reluctance. "But only because I refuse to let you run this project into the ground."

As we dove into the numbers, the atmosphere shifted, tension gradually morphing into a strange camaraderie. Our discussions became a dance of witty exchanges and sharp insights, each of us pushing the other to explore new angles and consider possibilities we hadn't before.

I found myself laughing at his dry jokes, and for a moment, the barrier I'd built around my heart began to weaken. It was alarming how easily I slipped into this rhythm with him, a rhythm that felt surprisingly natural. But just as I began to revel in the unexpected connection, a voice broke the moment.

"Avery!" It was Lila, my boss, her tone laced with urgency as she burst into the room. "We need you in the conference room. Now."

My heart sank, the world shifting abruptly as reality crashed back in. I exchanged a look with Mason, and the warmth we'd just shared evaporated, replaced by the looming specter of our deadlines. "What is it?" I asked, following Lila out.

"There's been a development with the client," she said, glancing back at me, her expression grave. "They're unhappy with our progress and are threatening to pull out of the contract if we can't show significant improvements by the end of the week."

Panic clawed at my throat. "What? We've been working around the clock to meet their expectations!"

"Yes, but it seems our efforts aren't translating into the kind of results they want," she replied, urgency lacing her words. "We need a solid plan to reassure them before it's too late."

I entered the conference room, where several team members were already gathered, the atmosphere thick with tension and anxiety. Mason was there, and I felt the heat of his gaze on me as I took my seat. The table was cluttered with papers, laptops, and half-empty coffee cups—evidence of our collective struggle.

"Okay, everyone, let's brainstorm," Lila instructed, her voice commanding. "We need actionable solutions, and we need them fast."

As ideas bounced around the room, I glanced at Mason. He caught my eye, an unspoken understanding passing between us. In that moment, I realized that even in the midst of chaos, we were stronger together.

But just as we started to find our footing, the doors swung open again, this time revealing a figure I hadn't expected—our client's representative, a woman named Marissa with a reputation for being merciless. "I'm here for an update," she stated coolly, her gaze sweeping over us with a hawk-like intensity.

A hush fell over the room, and I felt my heart race as I turned to Mason, the weight of the situation crashing down on us. "Well, this is just delightful," I muttered under my breath, panic creeping in as Marissa took a seat at the head of the table, her expression unreadable.

"I trust you all are prepared to explain why we should continue our partnership," she said, her tone sharp as a knife, cutting through the tension like butter.

Mason leaned forward, confidence radiating from him, but I could sense the apprehension beneath his bravado. "Absolutely. We've been working diligently to meet your expectations—"

Before he could finish, Marissa held up a hand, her eyes narrowing. "I've seen your progress reports. They don't reflect the urgency I was expecting."

The atmosphere grew heavy, a storm brewing in the room as the reality of our situation loomed over us. I could feel the walls closing in, the pressure mounting, and I fought the urge to look at Mason for reassurance. We were in the trenches now, and failure was not an option.

As the meeting progressed, it became clear that our usual tactics wouldn't suffice. Each attempt to placate Marissa fell flat, and I could see the tension crackling in the air like static electricity. My mind raced, searching for a way to turn the tide.

"Mason," I whispered, leaning closer as the conversation shifted, "we need to take a risk. What if we propose a more aggressive timeline, show them our commitment?"

He hesitated, weighing the options as Marissa's impatience grew. "Are you sure? It could backfire if we can't deliver."

"If we don't make a move, we're done for," I urged, feeling the weight of desperation in my chest. "We can't let them see us falter."

Mason met my gaze, a spark igniting in his eyes. "Alright. Let's do it."

As he stood to address Marissa, the room held its breath, anticipation mingling with anxiety. "Marissa, we'd like to propose an adjusted timeline that ensures you'll see significant results much sooner. We believe this will demonstrate our dedication and commitment to this partnership."

Marissa's eyes flickered with intrigue, but before she could respond, the fire alarm suddenly blared, the shrill sound piercing through the tension like a dagger. Chaos erupted as people scrambled to their feet, confusion clouding the air.

I glanced at Mason, whose expression mirrored my own shock. "What the hell?" I exclaimed, grabbing his arm as we both started to move toward the exit.

"This is not happening," he muttered, the urgency palpable in his voice as we surged through the door, following the crowd toward the stairwell.

"Do you think it's a drill?" I shouted over the cacophony, adrenaline coursing through me.

"Not likely," he replied, urgency twisting his features. "We need to get everyone outside."

As we descended the stairs, the tension from earlier mingled with a sense of dread. Something about this felt wrong. I glanced back at Mason, the firelight casting shadows on his determined face, and my heart raced with uncertainty.

What awaited us outside? Would we emerge into chaos or something more sinister? In that moment, I realized that whatever was happening would change everything, and we were on the brink of an unknown future, our fates intertwined in a way I hadn't anticipated.

The door swung open, and the heat of the flames licked at the air around us, a reminder that the battle was far from over

Chapter 5: The Unexpected Ally

The soft glow of the café's pendant lights flickered like distant stars, casting a warm halo around the crowded room. I sat at my usual table in the corner, cradling a ceramic mug filled with rich, dark coffee that spilled warmth into my palms. The air buzzed with conversations—a symphony of laughter and clinking cutlery, weaving a tapestry of lives intersecting for just a moment. As I took a sip, the bitterness lingered on my tongue, a welcome distraction from the turmoil swirling in my mind.

Mason's voice, deep and textured like the coffee itself, sliced through the chatter. "You really think they're going to give you a better deal just because you asked nicely?" His words hung in the air like the sweet scent of pastries, instantly drawing my attention. He stood at the counter, his tall frame blocking the view of the barista as he leaned casually against the marble surface, the evening light catching the angles of his jaw and the soft sheen of his dark hair. I couldn't help but admire the way he commanded attention, even when he wasn't trying.

"I don't see why not," I shot back, a playful challenge dancing on my lips. "I believe in the power of charm." The words left my mouth before I could reconsider, and I cursed myself for revealing any vulnerability. Mason was the kind of man who thrived on dissecting weaknesses, and I had no intention of giving him any ammunition.

"Charm won't cut it when they're eyeing your spreadsheets and those projections," he replied, a smirk playing at the corners of his mouth. "They're in it for the profit, not your charm. You need to show them the numbers." The laughter around us dimmed as I focused solely on him. His nonchalance was infuriating and strangely alluring.

"Maybe," I said, attempting to sound indifferent. "But numbers can be manipulated. Besides, charm adds a little spice." I leaned back, taking another sip of my coffee, desperate to divert my mind from the unsettling heat igniting my cheeks. I wondered if Mason could sense the tremor in my voice, that subtle shift when I ventured too close to personal truths.

"Spice doesn't hold up in a boardroom," he countered, stepping closer, his presence enveloping me like a thick fog. "And when they see your sales pitch, they'll know you're all about the numbers, too."

"Wow, what a supportive friend you are," I quipped, rolling my eyes, though the tension between us felt tangible, like a tightrope strung high above an abyss. Was it just me, or was he leaning in just a fraction more?

Just then, the café door swung open, and a chill gust whipped through, carrying with it a few stray leaves and an unwelcome reminder of the world outside. A client, one I'd been dreading, strolled in, her eyes scanning the room until they locked onto mine. I stiffened, my heart racing. This was the last person I wanted to see right now, especially after the disaster that had unfolded during our last meeting.

"Hey, isn't that your boss's wife?" Mason murmured, his gaze shifting from me to the approaching figure. "What's her name—Linda?"

My stomach dropped as I caught sight of Linda's perfectly coiffed hair and sharp blazer, each detail an echo of her high-strung demeanor. I had barely survived our last encounter, where her icy critique left me reeling. "Yes, and she's definitely here for an unscheduled chat," I replied, my voice barely above a whisper.

"Mason!" she called out, her tone dripping with a false sweetness that sent a shiver down my spine.

Just as I considered slipping out the back door, Mason straightened, an unexpected resolve sharpening his features. "Stay here," he said, his tone firm yet low. "I'll handle it." Before I could protest, he sauntered toward her, every step infused with a confidence that both astonished and terrified me.

"Linda," he greeted, his voice smooth, a silk thread weaving through the air. "Fancy seeing you here. What brings you out tonight?"

I shifted in my seat, my heart thudding in a chaotic rhythm as I strained to hear their conversation. The way he spoke to her, effortlessly dismantling her icy facade, made me rethink everything I thought I knew about him. It was like watching a maestro conducting a symphony, each gesture precise and calculated, yet filled with an undercurrent of charm.

"Just a little gathering," she replied, her tone almost too saccharine. "I'm surprised to see you here, though. Shouldn't you be working late?"

He chuckled, a sound rich and inviting, and I felt an unexpected surge of admiration. "Oh, I like to mingle with the real talent when I can." There was a twinkle in his eye, and I could see Linda faltering, her expression wavering between irritation and intrigue.

The tension crackled as I watched them interact, wondering how this moment would unfold. Mason had turned the tables, shifting the power dynamic in a way I hadn't anticipated. He was no longer just the handsome antagonist in my narrative; he was a formidable ally, one who might just shield me from my mounting anxieties.

Linda's posture relaxed slightly, her eyes flickering back toward me, clearly sizing up the situation. "And what about your little project with Sarah? How's that going?"

Mason waved a dismissive hand, expertly deflecting her question. "Oh, it's just a side project. You know how it is—some people need a little extra push." He glanced back at me, a quick flash of understanding passing between us. "But I'm more interested in your thoughts on the recent merger. Quite the news, isn't it?"

In that moment, I realized something remarkable. The world of numbers and spreadsheets, of power plays and corporate hierarchies, could sometimes be softened by the unexpected warmth of camaraderie. Mason's casual bravado was more than mere charm; it was a lifeline, an assurance that I wasn't navigating these treacherous waters alone.

As Linda floundered under his onslaught of questions, I couldn't help but feel a growing affection for this man who seemed to revel in challenging the status quo, even if it meant stepping outside his own carefully crafted persona. There was something inherently beautiful about the way he dismantled the tension, turning it into a dance of wits.

For a fleeting moment, as I watched him handle Linda with grace and cunning, I allowed myself to dream of what it might mean to have a partner in this relentless game. Someone who could match my ambition and, maybe, just maybe, offer a bit of warmth along the way.

But just as quickly as that thought took root, I buried it deep within the walls I'd built. There was a mission at hand, and I couldn't afford to get lost in the haze of infatuation, no matter how compelling Mason's presence was. He was an ally, and I needed to keep it that way.

The café hummed with life as I settled back into my seat, the remnants of Mason's unexpected intervention swirling in my thoughts. I could still see him standing tall, effortlessly deflecting Linda's sharp comments, his expression poised yet playful. That moment had sparked something within me, a flicker of curiosity about the man who had carved a path through my carefully constructed defenses. Yet, with each glance towards him, I felt the familiar tightening in my chest, a reminder of the delicate balance I needed to maintain.

"Coffee's not going to drink itself," Mason said, sidling back to my table, his mug in hand and that infuriatingly charming smirk still etched across his face. "You looked like you might need a refill after that little tête-à-tête." He slid into the chair opposite me, the tension in his body palpable, as though he were still brimming with the adrenaline of our encounter.

"Thanks for the save," I replied, trying to keep my tone light, though the warmth of gratitude settled like a gentle weight in my stomach. "I thought I was going to drown in her expectations."

"Expectation is just disappointment waiting to happen," he quipped, raising an eyebrow as he sipped his coffee. "So, what's the plan for next week? Are you still going to try to charm the numbers out of your clients?"

I rolled my eyes, yet the corner of my mouth betrayed me with a hint of a smile. "I'm serious! My strategy involves a delicate blend of charm and facts. You wouldn't understand."

"Delicate? You? I can't imagine." His voice dripped with sarcasm, and I couldn't help but laugh, a sound that felt foreign yet liberating.

"Okay, fair point," I admitted, leaning in slightly, eager to bridge the gap between our banter and something more substantial. "But it's not like you're the expert on subtlety either. You strutted in there like you owned the place."

"I just prefer to take control when I can," he replied, an enigmatic glimmer in his eye. "Especially when someone's about to get skewered by a corporate predator."

The playful exchange was interrupted as a group of friends entered the café, their laughter bright and infectious. I watched them for a moment, feeling an odd mixture of longing and envy. They were carefree, lost in their world, while I was tangled in a web of deadlines and expectations. "Must be nice to just... be," I murmured, my gaze still on the lively group.

Mason's expression softened slightly. "You don't have to be tied down by all that, you know. There's more to life than spreadsheets and projections."

"Oh, sure," I replied, waving my hand dismissively. "I'll just trade in my corporate ladder for a life of leisure. I hear 'being free' is a hot career choice."

His laughter danced around us, warm and rich, easing the weight on my heart. "Seriously, though, do you ever take a break? Like, actually stop and breathe?"

I hesitated, my defenses flickering as I considered his question. "It's hard to find the time. There's always something needing my attention."

"Life's a lot more enjoyable when you allow a little chaos in. You should try it sometime." His voice was sincere, coaxing me to venture into a territory I had long deemed dangerous. I was tempted, but I couldn't afford distractions.

"Chaos doesn't pay the bills," I replied, shaking my head.

"Neither does boredom," he shot back, his eyes sparkling with mischief. "But here we are."

We fell into a comfortable silence, the café's ambiance wrapping around us like a soft blanket. The clinking of dishes and murmured conversations faded into the background, leaving just the two of us in our little bubble of camaraderie. It was unnerving, this sudden ease between us, as if we were two characters drawn together by fate, defying the odds stacked against us.

"Do you ever think about what's next?" Mason's question cut through the moment, startling me. "Like, really think about it?"

"Next? As in the next promotion?" I replied, my voice a pitch higher than usual. "Why would I do that when I'm still trying to survive today?"

"Because today's just a stepping stone," he insisted, leaning forward, the intensity in his gaze making my breath catch. "If you're not careful, you'll wake up one day and wonder how you let life slip away."

His words struck a chord deep within me, reverberating like a bell tolling in the distance. I wanted to dismiss his concern, to scoff at the notion that my life was passing me by, but a part of me knew he had a point. I felt the weight of the ambitions I'd sacrificed on the altar of duty, the dreams I had shelved for the sake of practicality.

"I'll consider it," I said, trying to inject levity back into the conversation. "Right after I finish saving the world, one spreadsheet at a time."

He chuckled, the sound rich and full of life. "I'd pay to see that. You dressed as a superhero with a cape made of Excel sheets."

"Hey, it's a valid look," I protested, but we both knew I was deflecting. The laughter faded into an uneasy silence, each of us lost in our thoughts.

Just then, a commotion erupted at the entrance, pulling my attention away. A pair of newcomers, a couple clearly in the throes of an argument, stormed into the café. Their voices sliced through the ambient noise, raw and heated, creating an atmosphere thick with tension. "You never listen to me!" the woman shouted, her cheeks flushed with anger.

"Maybe because you never say anything worth hearing!" the man fired back, the words echoing through the café.

Mason and I exchanged glances, our light-hearted moment punctured by the brewing storm of conflict. "Well, this should be entertaining," he remarked dryly, tilting his head to watch the spectacle unfold.

"Should we intervene?" I whispered, suddenly feeling the weight of the unfolding drama.

Mason shrugged, an amused grin on his face. "Unless you want to add 'relationship counselor' to your resume, I'd say let them hash it out."

I snorted at the absurdity of that thought, yet I couldn't shake the feeling of unease settling in my stomach. "Maybe we should at least check if they need a mediator?"

"Do you think we're equipped for that?" he teased, his eyes sparkling with humor. "We can barely keep our own banter on track."

"Good point," I conceded, watching as the couple continued their verbal exchange, oblivious to the onlookers. "It's like watching a train wreck—you can't look away."

As the argument escalated, I felt an unexpected surge of empathy. The couple reminded me of myself in so many ways—caught up in their own worlds, struggling to be heard. "Maybe they just need someone to listen," I mused, my voice barely above a whisper.

"Or maybe they just need to step outside and take a breath," Mason suggested, his tone more serious now. "Sometimes a little distance does wonders for perspective."

"True," I replied, nodding slowly. "But how often do we actually do that?"

He smiled softly, and in that moment, I realized I wasn't just seeing him as a potential ally in my professional battles; I was starting to glimpse a man beneath the layers of sarcasm and bravado. A man who might understand the complexities of ambition, the longing for connection buried beneath the façade of independence.

The café buzzed around us, but our conversation felt like a fragile thread connecting two souls in a chaotic world. It was more than just coffee or casual banter; it was a moment of clarity, a step toward something neither of us had anticipated. Yet, as my heart raced with the thrill of possibility, a small voice in the back of my mind warned me to tread carefully. Life had a way of throwing unexpected curveballs, and I wasn't quite ready to catch one.

The argument at the café escalated, transforming the atmosphere into something almost tangible, like thick smoke curling around us. I shifted in my seat, caught between wanting to dive into the chaos and remaining in the sanctuary of my conversation with Mason. The couple's heated words crackled through the air, raw and unfiltered, revealing the depths of their frustrations. "You don't care about what I want!" the woman shouted, her voice rising above the hum of the café.

Mason leaned closer, his brow furrowing slightly. "You think we should intervene?" he asked, his tone shifting from playful to serious, as if contemplating a rescue mission.

"No, no, let them sort it out," I whispered, glancing over at the couple. "But it makes me think… what if they're like us? Just trying to figure things out, only to get lost in the noise?"

"Or they're just a couple of drama queens," Mason replied with a chuckle, but there was an undertone of understanding in his voice. "Still, it's fascinating to watch, isn't it? They might be learning something important about each other, or just demonstrating how not to communicate."

I couldn't help but laugh, the tension easing slightly. "Well, if they don't figure it out soon, I might need to step in. We've had enough real-life drama for one night."

Mason took a sip of his coffee, his eyes narrowing as he observed them. "You know, I was always told that conflict is the birthplace of clarity. Maybe they just need to push through the fire to come out the other side."

"Sounds poetic, but I'd prefer to stay on this side of the flames," I replied, and he grinned, the corners of his mouth curling up as he caught my gaze.

The couple continued their argument, oblivious to our distraction, and as I watched their faces twist with anger and hurt, I felt a strange sense of kinship with them. Wasn't that how it often felt—like you were fighting to be heard in a world that constantly drowned you out? I opened my mouth to share my thoughts, but before I could, the argument reached a fever pitch. "You're so selfish! It's always about you!"

"Selfish? You're the one who never listens!" the man shot back, his voice shaking with frustration.

I exchanged a glance with Mason, our expressions mirroring a mix of disbelief and empathy. "They're not even making a point anymore," I murmured. "It's all just noise."

"Maybe they need a third-party perspective," Mason suggested, a mischievous glint in his eye. "You know, like a love consultant."

"Are you volunteering?" I laughed, but my amusement was short-lived as the couple suddenly fell silent, their eyes darting around the café as if just realizing they had an audience. My heart raced; I was rooted to my chair, unsure whether to look away or lean in closer.

Then, unexpectedly, the woman's gaze fell on me, piercing and accusatory. "What are you staring at?" she snapped, her voice sharp as a knife.

"Um, not you," I stammered, heat flooding my cheeks. "Just... enjoying the atmosphere?"

Mason's chuckle echoed beside me, and I shot him a warning look, half-amused, half-terrified. But the moment of levity faded quickly. The man stepped closer to the table, his face a storm of emotion, and I could feel the tension radiating off him like heat from a fire.

"You think this is a joke?" he demanded, directing his ire not just at me but at the entire café. "You think this is some kind of entertainment?"

"No, I—" I started, but the words tangled in my throat, frustration and sympathy wrestling within me.

"Just back off!" the woman interjected, her eyes flashing. "You don't know anything about us!"

The tension coiled tighter around us, and Mason's hand shot out, resting lightly on my wrist, a silent reminder that I wasn't alone in this mess. The connection sent a jolt of reassurance through me, grounding me amidst the chaos.

"Hey, everyone," Mason interjected, his voice steady and calm, cutting through the rising tide of hostility. "No one's here to judge. We've all had rough days. Why don't you take a breather?"

The couple exchanged glances, and for a moment, the air hung heavy with uncertainty. The woman's expression softened just a fraction, a crack in her armor, but the man remained rigid, his fists clenched at his sides. "We don't need your advice," he said, though his voice lacked conviction.

"Maybe not," Mason replied smoothly, "but it might help to talk about it. Why not start there?"

I admired his confidence, the way he held the space between us, unflinching. "Sometimes talking it out is better than fighting it out," I added, surprised by my own boldness.

The couple paused, the fire between them dimming ever so slightly. "What do you know about it?" the woman asked, her defensiveness faltering.

"More than I care to admit," Mason quipped, leaning back in his chair with a casual air, as if he were merely recounting a funny story. "I've watched enough relationships blow up to know that sometimes, stepping away from the flames is the best way to avoid getting burned."

My admiration for him surged again, coupled with a hint of something deeper—could he really be this insightful, or was it just a façade?

As the couple exchanged wary glances, I felt a strange tension unspooling between us, something electric. In that moment, I realized how vulnerable we all were, how each of us carried our battles, the weight of unspoken words hanging in the air.

"Maybe we should go," I suggested softly, trying to alleviate the mounting awkwardness. "This isn't our fight."

"Just one more minute," Mason murmured, his attention fixed on the couple. "You guys seem like you have a lot to say. Why don't you start from the beginning?"

The woman opened her mouth, her lips trembling, but just as she seemed ready to speak, the café door swung open again. A chilling breeze swept through, carrying the unmistakable tension of an approaching storm. In stepped a newcomer, someone who seemed out of place, yet entirely at home among the chaos.

"Hey, Mason! Fancy seeing you here!" The voice was familiar, yet laced with an undertone that sent my pulse racing. I turned, and my heart sank at the sight.

Standing there with a triumphant smirk was my former colleague, Jenna, the very person I'd hoped to avoid. She was a force of nature, with her striking red hair and sharp wit, and the last thing I needed was her unfiltered commentary on the state of my life.

"What are you doing with them?" Jenna motioned toward the couple, her tone dripping with intrigue as she eyed Mason and me with unmistakable delight. "Are you playing mediator now?"

The couple exchanged glances again, confusion flickering across their faces as they tried to decipher the newcomer's intentions. My heart raced as the tension shifted, the café buzzing with renewed energy and the promise of drama. I wanted to sink into my chair and disappear, but I knew that wasn't an option.

"Jenna, not now," I said, a hint of urgency creeping into my voice.

But she only grinned wider, stepping further into the café, her presence electrifying the air. "Oh, but I think now is exactly the right time!"

And just like that, the thread of camaraderie that Mason and I had woven began to unravel, the fragile connection exposed to the merciless gaze of the world outside. My heart hammered as I sensed that the coming moments would change everything, unraveling the delicate tapestry we had begun to weave in our corner of the café. The unexpected ally I had come to rely on now stood on the brink of revelation, and I couldn't shake the feeling that this was just the beginning of something far more complicated than either of us had anticipated.

Chapter 6: The Warning

The tension between us had become a palpable thing, a thin thread stretched taut in the air, ready to snap at any moment. I could feel it coiling around my heart each time Mason entered the room, his presence a magnet pulling me closer yet leaving an unmistakable chill in its wake. He moved with an effortless confidence, his broad shoulders brushing against the edge of my cluttered desk as he leaned in, his breath warm against my ear. Yet the warmth felt tinged with an unsettling chill, one that mirrored the uncertainty brewing in my gut.

The world around us pulsed with energy, the dim lights of the office flickering like nervous fireflies as I tried to focus on the spreadsheet sprawled before me, columns of numbers blurring into an incomprehensible haze. Then, amidst the familiar chaos of deadlines and client meetings, I found it—an innocuous white slip of paper resting on my desk, as out of place as a snowflake in July. My heart skipped as I reached for it, the edges crisp and unyielding against my fingertips.

"Know who you trust." The words echoed in my mind like the tolling of a bell, each syllable heavy with unspoken implications. The room seemed to constrict around me, walls inching closer as if they shared my growing sense of dread. I could practically hear the gears grinding in my mind, spinning with the possibility that I was in deeper than I had ever anticipated.

"Everything okay?" Mason's voice broke through my thoughts, and I looked up, momentarily startled by the intensity of his gaze. His brow furrowed, concern mingling with something darker that I couldn't quite place. The light caught the sharp angles of his jaw, casting him in an almost predatory light. He was a lion in a well-tailored suit, and I was just a gazelle, aware that the hunt was always on, even if I was too stubborn to run.

I forced a smile, hoping to deflect his scrutiny. "Just an odd note," I said, my voice deceptively light. "You know how it is—office pranks and all."

Mason's eyes narrowed slightly, suspicion flickering across his features. "What does it say?"

"It's nothing," I insisted, folding the paper and tucking it away, as if by doing so I could erase the threat lingering in the air. "Just a reminder to be careful. You know how this place can get." I didn't want to burden him with my fears, but a part of me desperately wanted to share, to lay bare my worries like a confession on the altar of our uneasy connection.

He stepped closer, the scent of his cologne—a mix of cedar and something earthy—washing over me, sending my heart racing for all the wrong reasons. "If someone's trying to intimidate you, I want to know. I can handle it." His tone was deceptively calm, but I sensed the storm brewing just beneath the surface. There was a fire in his eyes, a fierce protectiveness that sent warmth rushing through me even as it made the air grow heavier with tension.

I hesitated, the note weighing heavily in my pocket, the words haunting my thoughts. "You don't have to handle everything, Mason. You have enough on your plate without worrying about—"

"About you?" he interrupted, a smirk tugging at his lips, a playfulness battling against the seriousness of the moment. "You're part of my plate now. So, I'll worry as much as I damn well please."

The vulnerability in his expression was disarming, cutting through the fog of fear that clung to me. I wanted to argue, to insist I could take care of myself, but the truth was, the stakes had never felt higher. With rivals circling like vultures, I knew Mason's world was a chessboard, and I was just a pawn who had stumbled into the game without knowing the rules.

"Okay," I finally conceded, my heart thudding in a rhythm that felt both exhilarating and terrifying. "Just promise me you'll be careful. I don't want to lose you in this... mess."

His smile faded, the gravity of my words sinking in. "I promise," he said, though there was a weight in his voice that made me question how truthful that promise could be.

The rest of the evening slipped by in a blur, the tension woven into every glance and gesture. I went through the motions of work, the office sounds muted against the cacophony of my racing thoughts. When the clock struck six, the decision to leave felt both liberating and suffocating. I found myself half-hoping he would ask me to stay, to break the tension with more playful banter, yet I sensed he needed to distance himself from the growing shadows.

As I stepped out into the cool evening air, the bustling city wrapped around me, its vibrancy contrasting sharply with the weight settling in my chest. Streetlights flickered, casting a golden hue on the pavement, and I walked, one foot in front of the other, mind racing. The note in my pocket felt like a ticking bomb, each heartbeat reminding me that danger could be lurking behind every corner.

I glanced back at the office building, its darkened windows reflecting the gathering night, and a shiver ran down my spine. Was I safe? The thought echoed ominously in my mind as I navigated through the throngs of people, their laughter and chatter a distant hum compared to the silence creeping into my heart.

It was then that I noticed the figure standing across the street, leaning against a lamppost, shrouded in shadow. I hesitated, my instincts screaming at me to move, to turn back and seek the safety of the office, but curiosity anchored my feet to the ground. The figure raised their head slightly, the glint of a familiar smile catching the light, and recognition shot through me like a bolt of lightning. It was someone I had hoped never to see again, their presence a chilling reminder of the dangers lurking beneath the surface of my new life.

A chill ran through me, the kind that doesn't just nudge but shoves you into a cold, dark corner of your mind where paranoia thrives. I was rooted to the spot, staring across the street at the figure whose presence sent an icy shiver skittering down my spine. The lamppost illuminated just enough of their face to reveal a sly grin, one that hinted at mischief and malice. Jamie. My ex. The very definition of bad news wrapped in a pretty package, and here he was, beckoning me back into a world I thought I had escaped.

"Fancy seeing you here," he called out, his voice dripping with that familiar mix of charm and danger. He pushed himself off the lamppost, strolling toward me with an easy confidence that reminded me all too well of why I had fallen for him in the first place. He had a way of making even the most mundane moments feel like an adventure. But now? Now it felt like a trap.

"Jamie," I said, forcing my voice to remain steady, though every instinct screamed at me to run. "What are you doing here?"

He shrugged, hands tucked casually into his pockets, a nonchalant grin stretching across his face. "Just passing through. You know how it is—life is one big highway, and sometimes you run into old friends at unexpected rest stops."

"Old friends?" I echoed, the words tasting bitter on my tongue. "I wouldn't classify you as a 'friend' after everything."

"Touché." He stepped closer, the distance between us shrinking as he studied me with those mischievous eyes that had once made my heart race. "But you have to admit, I do have a knack for showing up at just the right moment."

I folded my arms defensively, aware of how futile it was to resist the tide of memories crashing against my resolve. "And this is what you call a 'right moment'? Because I'm pretty sure I was doing just fine before you decided to stroll back into my life."

"I missed you, you know." The sincerity in his tone was disarming, and for a brief second, the girl who had fallen for his smooth talk began to surface. But that girl was buried deep under layers of self-preservation, and she was fighting hard to stay there.

"Right. And is that why you're here, to pull me back into your chaos? Because I've had enough of that for one lifetime." I couldn't ignore the way my heart quickened, or how his words wrapped around me like a warm blanket, tempting but dangerous.

"Chaos?" He laughed, a sound that rolled over me like thunder. "You think I bring chaos? Oh, honey, you haven't seen chaos until you've met some of the characters in Mason's little entourage."

The mention of Mason brought a flash of heat to my cheeks, and I felt a strange protectiveness surge within me. "Mason isn't chaos; he's—"

"—a player in a much bigger game, I know." Jamie cut me off, his voice dropping to a conspiratorial whisper. "But don't you see? You're in the middle of a storm. And I'm the only one who knows how to navigate the waters."

My stomach twisted, a cocktail of anger and anxiety swirling within me. "And what makes you think I'd ever trust you again? You had your chance, and you blew it."

He stepped closer, his gaze intense. "Trust isn't always a choice. Sometimes it's a necessity."

I wanted to scoff, to tell him he was being ridiculous, but there was a kernel of truth in his words that struck too close to home. I was standing at the crossroads, and both paths were fraught with peril. "What do you want, Jamie?"

"Just to talk," he replied, the tone of his voice shifting, losing some of that playful edge. "But not here. Not out in the open where prying eyes can eavesdrop. Let's grab a drink, just like old times. I promise I won't bite."

I hesitated, a war raging inside me. The idea of going anywhere with him felt reckless, yet I couldn't shake the instinct that his presence could serve as a kind of twisted lifeline, or maybe a trap set to ensnare me. "I don't think that's a good idea," I finally said, the words tumbling out more firmly than I felt.

"Why not? Afraid I'll steal your secrets?" he quipped, raising an eyebrow. "Or is it that you're worried Mason might hear? I have a feeling he's not quite the knight in shining armor you think he is."

The mention of Mason twisted something inside me, but I swallowed down the protest rising to my lips. "Mason is nothing like you, Jamie. He's a good man."

"Is he?" Jamie's voice lowered, dripping with skepticism. "Good men get people hurt, you know. They have that way of making promises they can't keep."

"Unlike you?" I shot back, venom dripping from my words. "Because you've been a paragon of honesty in the past."

"Touché again." He smirked, a hint of respect glimmering in his eyes. "But I'm not the one you should be worried about. I came to warn you, not to rehash the past. Mason's got enemies, and I'm not talking about the petty squabbles you hear about in the office."

Each word felt like a weight pressing down on me, suffocating the air. "What are you talking about?"

"Let's just say, not everyone appreciates his rise to power. There are those who wouldn't think twice about using you as a pawn to get to him."

A chill crept up my spine again, the pieces of a puzzle I hadn't realized I was working on suddenly coming together in a jumbled mess. "So, you're here to help? Or are you just trying to manipulate the situation for your own benefit?"

"Maybe a little of both," he admitted, his honesty disarming. "But you have to see the bigger picture. People like Mason don't play by the same rules. If you're not careful, you'll end up in a position you can't escape from."

My thoughts raced, grappling with the storm of information crashing against the walls I had built around my heart. Could he be telling the truth? Could Mason's world be more dangerous than I had been led to believe?

"Why should I believe anything you say?" I challenged, struggling to keep my voice steady, but the uncertainty was creeping back in, wrapping around me like a noose.

"Because I'm here now, and I don't want to see you get hurt," he said, a flash of sincerity breaking through his usual bravado. "Whether you believe it or not, I care about you."

It was a dangerous declaration, one that flickered with the potential for both truth and treachery. I could feel the pull of his words, but just as quickly, I felt the repulsion of everything he had ever done. "You don't get to say that after everything," I snapped, anger flaring to life.

He raised his hands in mock surrender. "Alright, fair point. But let's not pretend you're not curious. How many times have you thought about our past? How many times have you wondered what could have been?"

"Not enough to want to drag you back into my life," I shot back, though my heart betrayed me, memories of our laughter swirling with the darkness of our parting.

"Then let's talk about your future. You're playing a dangerous game, and you need someone who knows the rules."

"You think you're that person?"

"I might be your best shot at survival."

The tension between us crackled with unresolved energy, every word hanging heavy in the air. A part of me wanted to walk away, to brush off his charm as just that—charm. But another part, one that thrived on the thrill of the unknown, was intrigued. As I stood there, faced with the remnants of our history and the shadows looming on the horizon, I was torn between the safety of the known and the reckless allure of the unpredictable.

The air between us was thick with unsaid words, tension weaving through the fabric of our conversation as Jamie leaned against the lamppost, his demeanor shifting from playful to something more serious. I could see the flicker of determination behind his charming facade, and it unsettled me more than I cared to admit. He was like a chess piece—strategically placed, always considering the next move. "Listen," he said, lowering his voice as if afraid of being overheard, "I wouldn't come to you unless I thought it was important."

"Then let's hear it," I replied, my voice sharper than I intended. The last thing I wanted was to feel like I was being drawn into another one of Jamie's schemes, but something in his eyes hinted at urgency that felt impossible to ignore.

"Mason's connected to people who play dirty. You know that, right?" Jamie's words hung in the air, heavy and foreboding. "I've seen it firsthand. He's not just another businessman trying to make a name for himself. He's in deep, and the deeper you get, the harder it is to breathe."

"Is that supposed to scare me?" I shot back, crossing my arms defensively. "Because it's not working."

He stepped closer, the space between us narrowing until the faint smell of his cologne—a mix of leather and cedar—wrapped around me like an unwanted embrace. "I'm not trying to scare you. I'm trying to protect you. There are whispers, rumors that he's not as loyal as he appears. The kind of loyalty that's only skin deep."

I felt a chill as his words sank in, the echoes of doubt clawing at the edges of my mind. "And you're the expert on loyalty, right? After everything?"

"Fair point." He raised his hands in mock surrender, a smirk dancing on his lips. "But sometimes, the ones who know the most about betrayal are the ones who've experienced it firsthand."

I searched his face for any hint of deceit, but all I saw was an unsettling mixture of sincerity and desperation. "Why do you care so much? You made your choice to walk away from me."

"Because I care about you, damn it!" His voice rose, frustration threading through his tone. "You might not see it now, but you're in over your head. I'd rather face the devil myself than watch you get caught in the crossfire."

The words hung in the air like a fragile ornament, ready to shatter at the slightest touch. I was torn between the warmth of his concern and the chill of his past, caught in a web of emotions that pulled me in every direction. "What do you want me to do?" I asked, my voice softer now, the fight draining out of me.

"Just consider your options. You can trust Mason, but you need to know exactly what you're trusting him with." His expression softened, and for a fleeting moment, the boy I had once loved peeked through the walls he had built around himself.

I was about to respond when the world around us seemed to shift. The bustling street noise dimmed, replaced by an eerie stillness that prickled at my skin. I glanced over Jamie's shoulder and froze. Mason stood a few paces away, his dark eyes locked on us, the expression on his face inscrutable.

"Is this a bad time?" he asked, voice steady, but the tension radiating from him was palpable.

Jamie's smirk vanished, replaced by a cautious neutrality that instantly raised the stakes. "We were just—"

"Having a very private conversation, I can see." Mason's gaze bore into me, the warmth of his presence now feeling like a cold, steel grip. "What are you doing with him?"

"I—" My words faltered, the uncertainty washing over me. There was no way to explain the complicated web of emotions without revealing far too much. "We were talking."

"About what?" Mason's voice sharpened, and I could feel Jamie's presence fade into the background, his previous bravado replaced by a wary watchfulness.

"Just old times," I said, forcing a casualness into my tone that felt anything but genuine. "Nothing that concerns you."

"Oh, but it does concern me," Mason countered, his eyes narrowing slightly, the intensity in them enough to make my heart race. "Anyone who has ever had a past with you concerns me, especially someone like him."

"Someone like me?" Jamie interjected, a glimmer of amusement creeping into his voice as if he were enjoying the tension between us far too much. "Careful, Mason. Sounds like you're trying to claim her as your territory."

Mason took a step closer, every muscle in his body tensed, the air thick with the promise of confrontation. "I'll do what it takes to protect what's mine, Jamie."

The silence stretched, an unspoken challenge hanging in the air. My pulse quickened, each beat echoing the weight of the moment. "Guys, let's not do this here," I interjected, desperate to defuse the situation. "This is ridiculous."

Jamie chuckled softly, eyes darting between us. "Oh, this is rich. I never thought I'd see the day when Mason would feel threatened."

Mason shot him a glare so fierce I thought it might set the night ablaze. "You should be the one worried, Jamie. You're stepping into something you don't understand."

"Maybe I'm just trying to help." Jamie shrugged, his bravado faltering under the intensity of Mason's stare.

"Help? By trying to worm your way back into her life?" Mason's voice dripped with disdain. "You have a funny definition of help."

"Stop," I said, my voice rising above the tension like a lifeline thrown into turbulent waters. "This isn't helping anyone. I'm not some prize to be won."

Mason's expression softened slightly, but his eyes remained steely, filled with a mix of protectiveness and frustration. "No one is saying you are, but I won't let anyone put you in danger. Not him, not anyone."

"Is that what you think? That I'm in danger?" I challenged, the remnants of fear creeping back in. "Or are you just trying to control me?"

His gaze pierced through me, and for a moment, I could see the battle within him. "It's not control; it's survival. I won't let you become a target, not when I can do something about it."

I glanced at Jamie, whose face had hardened into a mask of defiance, a smirk still lingering as if he found this all amusing. "This is all quite the spectacle, isn't it? But you both need to wake up and smell the coffee. I'm not here to steal anyone's thunder. I'm here because the storm is coming, and you're both standing in the eye of it."

"Enough of this," Mason said, his voice low and dangerous. "If you want to talk about storms, we can. But it'll be on my terms, not yours."

Jamie opened his mouth to retort, but before he could say another word, a loud crash erupted from down the street, echoing against the walls of the buildings and slicing through the tension that had thickened around us.

A sleek black car skidded to a halt, tires screeching against the asphalt, and I caught a glimpse of something glinting in the dim light—metal, a flash of steel. The hair on the back of my neck stood up as instinct kicked in, my heart pounding like a war drum.

"Mason!" I shouted, but before I could warn him, the door swung open, and a figure emerged, gun drawn, eyes scanning the crowd with predatory precision.

Time seemed to freeze, a heartbeat stretched into eternity. Mason moved instinctively, positioning himself in front of me, his body a shield against whatever threat loomed ahead. The world around us erupted into chaos, screams echoing through the night, drowning out the sound of my racing thoughts.

"Get down!" Mason barked, his voice a commanding roar that cut through the panic.

But I couldn't move, fear anchoring me in place as I stared into the face of danger, everything I thought I knew unraveling before my eyes. In that moment, I realized I was no longer just a spectator in this game; I was a player, and the stakes had never been higher.

Chapter 7: Unveiling the Shadows

The dim light of the bar flickered like the pulse of a hesitant heart, casting elongated shadows that danced across the worn wooden floor. I nestled deeper into my corner booth, the leather worn and cracked, much like the lives that slipped through its doors each night. The air hung heavy with the mingling scents of cheap bourbon and the stale remnants of last week's karaoke night, where off-key renditions of classics reverberated against the walls. I cradled my drink, the glass cool against my palm, as I scanned the crowd for anything unusual, any sign that my investigation might be bearing fruit.

It was hard to believe that just a week ago, I was blissfully unaware of the web of darkness entwined with Mason's life. The memories of our earlier encounters still lingered, his confident smirk and the way his dark eyes seemed to see straight through me. He was danger wrapped in charm, a stark contrast to the mundane existence I had known. Now, every conversation was laced with double meanings, every laugh an echo of something sinister lurking just beneath the surface.

"Still chasing shadows, are we?" The voice was smooth as silk, drawing my attention from the dimly lit bar to the figure standing beside my table. It was Nick, a familiar face from the precinct, his hands stuffed into the pockets of his leather jacket, his dark hair tousled like he had just rolled out of bed. I tried to ignore the flutter in my chest at his unexpected presence.

"Only the ones that seem to be stalking me," I shot back, my tone wry but playful. "You should know better than to sneak up on a girl investigating a mob boss. It's dangerous work."

"Mob boss?" he echoed, one brow raised in playful disbelief. "I thought you were writing a true crime novel."

"Very funny," I rolled my eyes, allowing myself a small smile. "I'm serious, Nick. There's more going on with Mason than meets the eye, and I intend to find out what it is."

"Good luck with that. He doesn't take kindly to curious people." His expression darkened for a moment, the playful glint fading. "And you definitely don't want to end up on his radar."

The warning hung in the air between us, thick as the smoke that swirled above our heads. I shrugged it off, unwilling to let fear dictate my actions. "If I don't chase the shadows, who will?"

Nick leaned closer, lowering his voice, the urgency clear in his tone. "Just promise me you'll be careful. This isn't some thriller novel where you get to play the hero and everything ends well."

"Since when did you become my personal guardian angel?" I quipped, but the edge of his concern gnawed at me.

"I'm not. But you matter, whether you believe it or not." He straightened up, a flicker of something I couldn't quite place in his eyes before he stepped back, creating distance that felt like a chasm. I glanced down at my drink, swirling the amber liquid, feeling the weight of his words settle into my bones.

With Nick's departure, I felt the bar's atmosphere shift, the noise of laughter and clinking glasses fading into a distant hum. I needed to refocus, to gather my thoughts on Mason and the tangled threads of his life that I was slowly unraveling. The whispers I had heard earlier at the precinct had teased something big, something buried beneath layers of deception and lies. I couldn't shake the feeling that I was on the precipice of something monumental.

Mason's world was painted in shades of gray, a stark contrast to the black and white morality I had always clung to. He walked that line effortlessly, charming yet intimidating, his presence demanding attention. I imagined him at his office, towering over his desk, surrounded by men who looked at him with a mix of reverence and fear.

As the evening wore on, I became absorbed in my thoughts, trying to piece together the puzzle of Mason's life. The more I learned, the more I realized that my initial fascination with him was just the tip of an iceberg that threatened to sink my little ship. Each whisper had led to a door I dared not open, a truth I was terrified to confront.

Suddenly, the door swung open, and a gust of cool night air rushed in, bringing with it a chill that sent shivers down my spine. I turned instinctively, the hairs on my arms standing at attention as my heart quickened. Mason stepped in, the unmistakable silhouette cutting through the dim light like a predator prowling its territory. He scanned the room, his eyes locking onto mine with an intensity that made my breath hitch.

"Mind if I join you?" His voice was low, gravelly, and impossibly smooth, sending a ripple of warmth through the chill that had settled in my bones.

"Sure," I managed, the cool demeanor I had built crumbling under the weight of his presence. He slid into the booth across from me, the air crackling with an energy I couldn't ignore.

"Been watching you," he said, a hint of amusement dancing in his eyes. "You're getting good at digging for dirt."

"I'm just gathering intel," I replied, unable to suppress a smirk. "You know, like a true detective."

He leaned in closer, the playful banter shifting to something more serious. "Just be careful. There are shadows even I don't want to chase."

His warning resonated, grounding me in a reality I was determined to navigate. As we sat in that dim bar, surrounded by the murmur of other patrons, the world outside seemed to fade away, leaving just the two of us tangled in a game where the stakes felt dangerously high.

The bar's warm light wrapped around us like a blanket, yet the conversation with Mason felt like a dance on a precipice, every word a step closer to the edge. His gaze was an intoxicating mix of challenge and allure, drawing me in as the world outside dimmed and faded. I took a sip of my drink, pretending the warmth in my chest was the whiskey and not the unspoken connection hanging between us.

"You really think you can just wade into the murky waters of my life without getting your feet wet?" Mason asked, leaning back slightly, a playful smirk dancing at the corners of his lips. The confidence radiating from him made my heart flutter, but I forced myself to match his bravado.

"Wet feet can dry, Mason. But ignorance is a much harder stain to clean," I shot back, determined to hold my ground. The thrill of our banter felt almost electric, like a game of chess where every move was crucial, and I was desperate not to lose.

He chuckled softly, the sound rich and warm. "Fair point. Just be mindful of the currents. Not everything that glitters is gold." The weight of his warning hung between us, each word laced with an unspoken history that intrigued me.

"Is that a warning or an invitation?" I replied, feigning nonchalance while internally reeling from his intensity. I couldn't help but wonder what hidden depths lay beneath that polished exterior.

"Depends on how you play it," he said, tilting his head slightly as if assessing my reaction. "But I assure you, the game isn't just about winning. Sometimes, it's about surviving."

His words wrapped around me like a shroud, igniting a mixture of fear and curiosity. I had stepped into a world filled with shadows, and Mason was both a guide and a potential threat. Each second I spent with him unveiled layers of complexity I hadn't anticipated, making it impossible to discern whether I was drawn in or trapped.

"Survival sounds exhausting," I said, my voice steady despite the turmoil beneath. "What do you do when you're tired of playing?"

Mason paused, his gaze piercing through the dim light, and for a moment, I saw something flicker in his eyes—a vulnerability that seemed at odds with the man I thought I knew. "You find a reason to keep going. Sometimes that reason is more dangerous than the game itself."

Intrigued, I leaned forward, the curiosity burning brighter than any caution. "And what's your reason?"

His smirk returned, but this time it was tinged with something deeper, more vulnerable. "Let's just say I have a few unfinished business dealings that require my attention."

"Business? Or something darker?" I pressed, my heart racing. I had opened Pandora's box, and now I was drawn to the chaos within.

"A little of both, I suppose," he replied, a trace of amusement dancing in his voice. "But it's not just about the business. It's about loyalty, power, and the lengths people will go to protect what they have."

"Sounds like you've got quite the soap opera going on."

"Don't forget the plot twists," he said, his eyes narrowing with a teasing glint. "Just when you think you know how it ends, someone pulls the rug out from under you."

The atmosphere shifted, the tension thickening like the humid air before a storm. My instincts screamed at me to retreat, yet I found myself leaning into the uncertainty, each revelation a thrill I couldn't resist.

"So, what's next? You're going to tell me you're involved in a high-stakes poker game?" I asked, trying to lighten the mood even as I sensed the gravity of our conversation.

"Not quite," he replied, his expression turning serious. "But I do have a meeting that could change everything."

A chill ran through me, the playful banter evaporating in the face of his intensity. "And you're telling me this now because…?"

"Because I need someone who can think outside the box, someone with guts."

"I have guts, Mason, but they come with a side of caution."

"Caution is overrated," he said, leaning closer, his voice dropping to a conspiratorial whisper. "Sometimes you have to dive into the chaos to find what you're looking for."

I met his gaze, the weight of his words settling in my chest. "And what if I don't like what I find?"

"Then you walk away. But I doubt you will," he replied, a challenge simmering just below the surface.

"Now you're just trying to bait me," I said, crossing my arms defiantly.

"Maybe I am. But I have a feeling you're not the type to back down."

I took a moment, weighing my options, the stakes suddenly feeling much higher. "So what's the plan? Am I supposed to follow you into whatever mess you've stirred up?"

A grin broke across his face, both playful and dangerous. "Exactly. And trust me, you'll want to be there when it all goes down."

I couldn't help but laugh, the absurdity of it all washing over me. "You really have a flair for the dramatic, don't you?"

"It's part of the charm," he replied, his tone mockingly serious.

"Right, the charming mob boss. Just what every girl dreams of."

"Not quite what I had in mind when I thought of romance," he said, smirking. "But you'd be surprised how thrilling danger can be."

With the lightheartedness lingering in the air, I felt a sense of resolve bubbling within me. "Alright, let's say I join you on this little adventure. What's the worst that could happen?"

"Famous last words," he murmured, his eyes sparkling with mischief.

But even as I spoke those words, I felt the familiar tingle of anxiety wrapping around my heart. I was stepping into a world that blurred the lines between danger and intrigue, and somehow, it was all tied to Mason.

As we leaned back in our seats, a moment of comfortable silence enveloped us, the chaos of the bar fading into the background. I realized I had crossed an invisible line, but for the first time, I felt an exhilarating thrill rush through me. The shadows I had been unraveling were not just Mason's—they were ours now, and I was more than ready to confront whatever darkness lay ahead.

The air around us crackled with unspoken tension, a heady mix of danger and intrigue. Mason leaned back, his confidence radiating like heat from a flame, and I could feel the challenge in his gaze, urging me to join him in the chaos he thrived in. "You've made your choice," he said, his voice smooth and steady, as if he held all the cards in our little game.

"Or maybe I'm just a glutton for punishment," I shot back, trying to mask the fluttering uncertainty that twisted in my gut. "What exactly is this adventure you've roped me into?"

His eyes danced with mischief, and I could see the corner of his mouth twitching as he fought a smile. "Just a little trip to meet some friends of mine. You'll love it, I promise."

"Friends? Or associates with dubious morals?" I couldn't help but probe, knowing full well that Mason's circle probably resembled a den of wolves more than a group of trustworthy allies.

"Consider it a networking opportunity," he said, his voice teasing, yet there was an undeniable edge to it. "You might even learn something that could help you in your little investigation."

"Right, because nothing says 'welcome' like a potential kidnapping," I replied, my sarcasm masking a genuine pulse of anxiety. Yet, there was an inexplicable thrill that rushed through me at the thought of stepping deeper into his world. "And where exactly are we going?"

"Somewhere we won't be disturbed," he said, his tone shifting to a more serious register. "Just trust me."

"Trust you? That's rich," I scoffed, but the challenge in his eyes was intoxicating. Every fiber of my being screamed caution, yet the magnetic pull toward Mason's world was overwhelming. I found myself wanting to know him better, to peel back the layers that cloaked his existence like a shroud.

As we exited the bar, the night air hit us with a cool embrace, sharp and refreshing against my flushed cheeks. Mason pulled a black leather jacket tighter around his broad shoulders, the moonlight casting shadows that danced along his features, deepening the contours of his jawline and emphasizing the dangerous allure he exuded.

"Get in," he said, gesturing to a sleek black car parked at the curb. My heart raced as I climbed in, the interior plush and inviting, yet I couldn't shake the feeling that I was stepping into a lion's den.

"Where's your driver?" I quipped, attempting to lighten the moment, though my pulse quickened at the thought of being utterly at his mercy.

"No driver tonight. Just you and me," he replied, a grin breaking through the facade. "Just like old times."

"Old times? Is this how you treat all your 'friends'?" I shot back, half-serious. The way he said it suggested an intimacy that both intrigued and unnerved me.

"You're not like the others," he said, his tone softer now, and for a moment, it felt as if we shared a secret just between us. But then he shifted gears, his voice becoming teasing again. "Besides, I promise I'll make it worth your while."

With that, he turned the key in the ignition, and the engine roared to life, vibrating with a pulse that matched my own racing heart. I watched the city lights blur past as we sped through the streets, the neon signs flickering like the chaos in my mind. Where was he taking me? What secrets awaited?

After a short drive, Mason pulled into a dimly lit alley, the kind of place that felt both secluded and menacing. The walls were draped in shadows, and the faint sound of music wafted through the air, heavy with bass. "This is it," he said, his voice dropping to a whisper as he turned off the engine.

"What, exactly, is 'it'?" I asked, glancing around nervously.

"Trust me. You'll understand soon enough," he replied, exiting the car and rounding to my side, offering his hand. I hesitated, looking at his outstretched palm as if it were a lifeline thrown into turbulent waters.

With a deep breath, I placed my hand in his, the warmth of his grip sending an unexpected thrill through me. Together, we made our way through a heavy wooden door that creaked ominously as it swung open, revealing a dimly lit room filled with smoke and laughter. The atmosphere felt charged, every whisper holding a hint of secrets waiting to be uncovered.

Inside, the space was a cross between a speakeasy and a clandestine meeting place—low lighting, plush couches, and a bar stocked with top-shelf liquor. A few tables were scattered about, and I could see groups engaged in quiet conversations, their tones hushed but urgent. The scent of cigar smoke hung in the air, mingling with something sweeter, almost intoxicating.

Mason led me to a table where several men and women sat, their expressions a mixture of amusement and curiosity. "Everyone, meet my intriguing guest," he announced, a hint of pride in his voice. "She's the one who's about to make this meeting a lot more interesting."

The group turned their attention to me, and I suddenly felt like a rabbit caught in the headlights, my heart racing as they sized me up. "Don't worry," Mason said, leaning in closer, "they bite, but it's nothing you can't handle."

"Great. Just what I needed," I muttered, trying to maintain my composure.

"Relax," he said, the glint in his eyes reassuring me, though I could sense the underlying tension. "You'll do just fine."

I took a seat, feeling the weight of their gazes as they shifted their focus back to Mason. The conversation quickly turned serious, veering into topics of deals, hidden assets, and shadowy transactions that made my head spin. I listened intently, piecing together fragments of information that painted a picture of Mason's world—a dangerous game filled with players who weren't afraid to go all in.

"Have you secured the package?" one man asked, his tone clipped and demanding.

"Working on it," Mason replied smoothly, his confidence unwavering. "But there are complications. Some people are getting curious."

"Curious people can be problematic," another voice chimed in, a woman with sharp features and an icy gaze. "You know what we discussed."

"I do," Mason said, his tone darkening. "But I won't risk losing what I've built over paranoia."

"Paranoia or caution?" the woman countered, raising an eyebrow.

"Caution has its merits," I interjected, surprising myself as I spoke up. All eyes turned to me again, the tension in the air thickening. "You can't just dismiss the potential threats. Ignoring them could lead to a catastrophic downfall."

The group exchanged glances, some impressed, others skeptical, but Mason's grin widened, clearly pleased with my boldness. "See? She gets it."

Before I could process the implications of what I'd just said, the atmosphere shifted abruptly. A door slammed open at the back of the room, and a figure entered, silhouetted against the light. The tension escalated, and my heart sank as I recognized the man stepping into the room.

"Looks like the party just got a little more complicated," Mason murmured, his voice low as he turned to face me, his expression a mix of surprise and concern.

The newcomer scanned the room with an icy glare, and I felt the weight of his gaze settle on Mason. "We need to talk," he said, his tone chilling the air around us.

Mason straightened, his demeanor shifting instantly from relaxed to guarded. "I wasn't expecting you," he said, the tension palpable.

"Clearly," the man replied, stepping forward. "But I'm here now, and we have a problem."

A chill ran down my spine, and I realized we had crossed into dangerous territory. The shadows that once felt exciting were now heavy with dread, a warning of the storm that was about to unfold. As I exchanged a glance with Mason, a silent understanding passed between us—this was just the beginning, and the game was far from over.

Chapter 8: The Broken Armor

The dim light of Mason's office cast shadows that danced along the walls, the air thick with the scent of leather and aged paper. It was a space filled with the quiet hum of authority—books lining the shelves like sentinels, each one a testament to his meticulous nature. I had entered with a fierce determination to address the latest contract clause that felt more like a trap than a negotiation. My heart raced as I prepared to confront him, fueled by a mix of frustration and trepidation.

"Mason," I began, my voice steadier than I felt. "We need to discuss the stipulations regarding—"

But the words faltered as I caught a glimpse of his expression. There was something in his eyes, a flicker of vulnerability that shattered the facade he wore so effortlessly. It was a chink in his armor, a glimpse of the man beneath the hardened exterior. He leaned back in his chair, fingers steepled, the usual confidence giving way to something more raw. It was a moment where the world outside faded away, leaving just the two of us in this sanctuary of secrets.

"I didn't expect to see you here after hours," he said, his voice low and gravelly, like distant thunder.

I shook my head, caught off guard by the intimacy of the moment. "Neither did I, but these clauses—"

"They're meant to protect us," he interrupted, the edge in his voice sharp enough to cut. Yet beneath the steel, I sensed a tremor, a flicker of something deeper—regret, perhaps, or the weight of memories he carried like a stone.

I could have pressed further, could have pushed him back into the corner where he was most comfortable, but instead, curiosity gnawed at me. "Protect us from what, Mason? What are you so afraid of?"

He flinched, the walls around him fortifying in an instant. The steel gaze returned, but there was a hesitation in his stance, an almost imperceptible shift that beckoned me closer. "You wouldn't understand."

"Try me," I challenged, my voice firmer now, laced with the urgency of my desire to breach that wall. "I might surprise you."

For a heartbeat, silence enveloped us, thick and heavy, pregnant with unspoken truths. Then, unexpectedly, he shifted, leaning forward, elbows resting on the desk. "Fine. But don't say I didn't warn you."

The words hung between us like a charged current, and I could feel the anticipation crackling in the air. "I'm listening."

With a sigh that seemed to come from the depths of his being, he began, his tone softer now. "When I was a kid, I thought I could change the world. I wanted to be a hero, you know? Save the day, that sort of thing." His eyes drifted away, lost in memories that played out like shadows behind his gaze. "But then… life happened."

"What happened?" I asked, my heart racing not just from his words but from the vulnerability they bore. I wanted to reach out, to touch the wound he was revealing, but I remained still, suspended in that moment.

He hesitated, a battle waging within him. "My brother," he finally said, his voice barely above a whisper. "He was my best friend, my partner in crime. We thought we were invincible until one day… we weren't." The words broke like glass, shattering the carefully constructed barriers between us.

"I'm sorry," I murmured, the empathy rushing in like a tide. I could see the boy he once was, the dreamer who had dared to hope amidst a landscape of hardship. "What happened to him?"

Mason's jaw tightened, and I could almost feel the chill emanating from him as he braced himself for the recollection. "He was in the wrong place at the wrong time. A mugging gone wrong. I should have been there. I could have stopped it." His fists clenched, and I noticed the way his knuckles paled against the dark wood of the desk, as if he were trying to hold onto the weight of his guilt.

The vulnerability in his confession tore at my heart, and the air felt charged with the gravity of his pain. "Mason, you can't blame yourself for that," I said softly, the words flowing from a place of understanding I hadn't known existed. "You were just a kid."

"Kids should know better. They should be able to protect the people they love." His voice hardened again, but beneath the steel was an echo of sorrow. It was a chasm that had defined him, a fracture that had carved out a piece of his soul.

The distance between us felt insurmountable, yet in that moment, I wanted to reach across the expanse, to offer solace where there was none. "You're not that little boy anymore. You've built this life, this empire. You're not alone."

His gaze snapped to mine, the heat of his intensity igniting a flame within me. "Maybe that's the problem. Maybe I've built these walls so high that I've forgotten how to let anyone in."

Our hands brushed against each other on the desk, and I felt an electric spark that jolted through me, a connection that transcended the weight of our shared burdens. Mason froze, and the air shifted, thickening with the weight of our unsaid words. In that trembling moment, I understood. He wasn't just my adversary; he was a man who had loved deeply and lost painfully, who had forged an unyielding armor around his heart to protect what remained.

The vulnerability in his gaze cracked something open within me, and I found myself drawn to him in a way I had never anticipated. It was dangerous, thrilling, and utterly terrifying all at once. I had come to confront him, but instead, we stood on the precipice of something far more profound, a shared understanding that felt like a fragile promise—a possibility that maybe, just maybe, we could find strength in our scars together.

The tension hung in the air like the sweet, heady scent of spring rain, promising renewal yet heavy with the remnants of old scars. I dared to linger in the charged silence, the soft brush of his fingers against mine still reverberating in my mind. It felt as if we were on the edge of something seismic, a revelation poised to shift the very ground beneath us. I inhaled slowly, as if the act alone might tether me to this moment, grounding me against the storm that had begun to brew in my chest.

"Mason," I ventured, my voice a soft thread amidst the unspoken weight. "You're more than your past. You know that, right?"

His gaze was a tempest, a blend of emotions I couldn't quite decipher—fear, longing, and something unnamable that sent a shiver racing down my spine. "You don't understand what it's like to carry those memories," he said, the hardness in his voice now laced with a reluctant sincerity.

"Try me," I replied, a flicker of defiance igniting within me. "I'm not as delicate as you think."

A wry smile tugged at the corners of his lips, a momentary lightness breaking through the storm clouds. "Delicate? You, with your relentless pursuit of truth and fairness? You're anything but delicate."

There it was—a connection forged from wit and understanding, like two pieces of a puzzle finally finding their place. The tension that had been suffocating us shifted, subtly yet profoundly. I dared to lean closer, emboldened by the truth we were sharing, as if each step forward drew us deeper into uncharted territory.

"Then what are we doing here?" I asked, tilting my head slightly to catch his gaze. "Why pretend that we're still just adversaries when this—" I gestured between us, "—is so much more complex?"

The intensity of his stare grew, unraveling the carefully woven threads of his defenses. "Maybe because it's easier to fight than to feel," he admitted, his voice a low murmur. "Fighting keeps me safe."

"Safe? Or just alone?" The question slipped from my lips, a gentle prod into the raw edges of his guarded heart.

He let out a harsh laugh, but it held no mirth. "Safety and solitude often dance hand in hand. You learn that quickly when you've seen too much."

The shadows on his face deepened, and I felt the urge to reach out again, to breach that distance that still lingered between us, invisible yet suffocating. "You've built these walls, Mason. But behind them, there's a man who's hurting. A man who deserves to heal."

"Maybe," he said, almost to himself. "But healing isn't a luxury I can afford."

"Who said anything about luxury?" I countered, my resolve hardening. "Healing is a necessity, Mason. You don't have to carry the weight of your brother's death alone. You can let it go."

A flicker of surprise danced in his eyes, as if my words had pierced through his armor in a way he hadn't expected. "You really think I can just let it go?" His voice was thick with disbelief, the remnants of his pain surfacing like ghosts from the past.

"I think you have to," I replied, the conviction in my voice surprising even myself. "Your brother wouldn't want you to be chained to his memory. He'd want you to live, to thrive."

Silence enveloped us once more, heavy and profound. I could see him grappling with the truth of my words, the weight of the past clashing with the flicker of hope. And in that moment, I realized that I wasn't just fighting for him. I was fighting for us—a possibility that flickered in the darkness like a beacon.

"Why do you care so much?" he finally asked, his expression shifting, revealing a vulnerability that shook me to my core.

"Because I see you, Mason," I replied, my voice softening. "I see beyond the steel walls and the contract negotiations. I see the man who's been hiding, who's been scared to show himself."

A hesitant smile broke through the tension, and I felt my heart skip at the sight of it. "Maybe you should run for office," he teased, but the warmth in his tone belied the lightness of his words.

"Maybe I should," I shot back with a grin, feeling the momentary levity envelop us like a warm embrace. But beneath the playful banter, there was an unspoken truth—an acknowledgment that this dance between us was no longer just a battle of wills. It was a fragile step toward something more, something profound.

"Tell me what you're really afraid of," I urged, my eyes locking onto his. "Is it about me? Or is it about you?"

His breath hitched, and the room seemed to shrink, the space between us pulsing with unfiltered emotion. "It's about everything," he said finally, his voice thick with raw honesty. "About trusting again. About letting someone in. It's terrifying."

"I won't betray your trust," I promised, the sincerity in my voice echoing like a solemn vow. "But you need to be willing to take that step."

He shifted, the weight of my words settling heavily upon him. "And if I can't?" His eyes bore into mine, searching for answers I wasn't sure I had.

"Then we take it together," I replied, my heart racing at the gravity of our connection. "One small step at a time."

A flicker of hope ignited in his gaze, and for the first time, I saw the faintest glimmer of light peeking through the cracks of his armor. It was as if he was beginning to believe that healing was possible, that trust could be earned. I could sense the fragile shift in the air, a quiet promise lingering between us.

"Okay," he said slowly, his voice steadier now, almost resolute. "Let's see where this goes."

A smile broke free on my lips, a mixture of relief and exhilaration flooding through me. The battle lines had shifted, the stakes higher than ever. I felt the warmth of his hand resting on the desk, an invitation, and I couldn't resist the urge to inch closer. There was still uncertainty, but the thrill of possibility surged between us, a dance of hope and healing that promised to weave our lives together in ways neither of us could have imagined.

As we sat there, on the precipice of something new, I knew the road ahead would be fraught with challenges and unexpected turns. But for the first time, the thought of facing them with Mason by my side didn't terrify me. It exhilarated me. And as the world outside continued its relentless march forward, we found ourselves enveloped in a cocoon of newfound connection, ready to forge a path through the darkness, together.

The moment lingered, stretching between us like the taut string of a bow, ready to snap at any provocation. I could feel my pulse quicken, not from fear but from the exhilarating uncertainty that swirled in the air. Mason's eyes held a tempest, a battle of emotions raging just beneath the surface. The barriers he had constructed with painstaking care now seemed poised to crumble, revealing a vulnerability that beckoned me to step closer.

"What happens now?" I asked, my voice barely above a whisper, as if louder words might shatter the delicate atmosphere we'd crafted.

His lips quirked into a reluctant smile, a fleeting crack in the armor he wore. "I suppose we keep talking. It seems we're both a bit better at that than fighting."

"Fighting is overrated anyway," I replied, a playful lilt to my tone that felt like a balm on the raw edges of our conversation. "Besides, who needs enemies when you have unresolved tension?"

"Is that what this is?" he shot back, a glimmer of challenge igniting in his gaze. "Unresolved tension?"

"Let's call it what it is: a delightful mess," I said, leaning back slightly, allowing the banter to dance between us. "It's far more entertaining than simply hurling insults at each other."

He chuckled, the sound rich and warm, breaking the chill that had hung over us. "I have to admit, you have a point. But you might want to keep your guard up. I can be a formidable opponent."

"Only if I let you," I teased, emboldened by the shift in our dynamic. "But I'm beginning to think you're not quite as fearsome as you want the world to believe."

"Ah, the daring detective thinks she's cracked the case," he countered, his voice laced with mock seriousness. "What else have you uncovered?"

"Let's see... you're a workaholic with a penchant for suffering in silence," I said, my eyes narrowing playfully. "And behind that icy exterior lies a heart that beats like a normal person's—full of fears, regrets, and maybe even a smidge of hope."

He raised an eyebrow, clearly intrigued. "Hope, you say? Isn't that a dangerous game?"

"It can be," I agreed, my tone turning serious for a moment. "But without it, what do we have left? Just a collection of missed opportunities."

His expression softened, the sharp lines of his face yielding to something gentler. "You really believe that?"

"Absolutely," I replied, my heart racing at the sincerity that swelled within me. "Life is too short to hide from what might be."

Mason leaned closer, the space between us narrowing as if drawn together by an invisible force. "And what might be?"

"This," I breathed, the air crackling with the weight of unspoken words and electrifying possibility. It was a moment suspended in time, a doorway to something profound. The distance melted away as our gazes locked, each of us caught in a web of attraction woven from shared vulnerabilities and blossoming trust.

Suddenly, a sharp knock at the door shattered the fragile bubble we'd created. The moment faltered, the warmth between us fraying as reality intruded with unforgiving force. Mason's gaze flickered toward the door, tension flooding back into his features.

"Damn it," he muttered, frustration etching lines into his brow.

"Should I hide?" I asked, half-serious, half-teasing, desperate to reclaim some of the intimacy we'd just forged.

"No," he said, shaking his head, but there was a flicker of uncertainty in his eyes. "It's... it's probably just the team wanting to discuss the contract."

"Right. Because that's what we do—put business before personal connections," I said, my voice laced with disappointment, though I tried to keep it light.

"Mason, it's me," a voice called from the other side, the familiar timbre belonging to Jake, his right-hand man. "We need your input on the logistics for tomorrow's pitch."

Mason's jaw tightened, and he glanced at me, the earlier warmth replaced with a sudden hardness. "I'll be out in a minute," he replied, his tone clipped.

"Are you serious?" Jake shot back, skepticism threading through his voice. "You're not going to pull another late night, are you? It's not good for your health."

I raised an eyebrow at Mason, a smirk creeping onto my lips. "Sounds like your team is worried about you."

"Let them worry," he said, frustration boiling beneath the surface. "They'll have to manage without me for a few minutes."

"Is that wise?" I asked, a playful challenge in my voice. "I mean, your team does seem to think you're some kind of corporate superhero."

"I'm just trying to figure out how to be a decent human being," he said, a glimmer of vulnerability returning to his gaze. "And that's proving to be more complicated than I thought."

Jake knocked again, this time more insistent. "Mason, come on! We need you. Don't make me come in there!"

Mason sighed heavily, the weight of leadership settling back on his shoulders. "You should probably go," I suggested gently, feeling the bittersweet pang of reality creeping back in. "They might actually need you."

His eyes held mine for a lingering moment, a silent conversation passing between us. "You're right. But I don't want to lose this." His gesture encompassed the intimacy we had shared, and I felt a warm rush at his words.

"Then don't," I replied, the determination in my voice firm. "You can have both—a thriving career and meaningful connections. Just take that leap."

He drew a deep breath, and the moment stretched, but the sound of Jake's impatience brought us crashing back to reality. With a reluctant sigh, Mason stood up, the energy between us shifting once more, back toward the businesslike formality that had initially defined our interactions.

"Fine," he said, his tone still laced with frustration. "But this isn't over."

"I wouldn't dream of it," I said, my smile playful yet sincere, hoping to reassure him as he opened the door, the creak of the hinges signaling a return to the everyday world.

Jake stepped in, his brow furrowing as he took in the scene, his eyes darting between us. "What's going on? Were you two having a moment?"

"It was nothing," Mason replied, the steel returning to his demeanor, but the way he glanced back at me told a different story. "Just discussing strategy."

"Right," Jake said, unconvinced. "Because you look like you've just come back from a walk in the clouds."

Mason shot me a look that was both playful and earnest, the fleeting connection still simmering in the air between us. "We'll talk later," he promised, his gaze holding mine, a lingering promise that sent a shiver of anticipation through me.

As he turned to focus on Jake, I felt a sudden pull of longing. I was just about to leave when I caught the glint of something in Mason's desk drawer—a flash of steel that sent a jolt of alarm through me. Before I could process it, the door swung open, and the tension in the room snapped back to the surface.

"What is it?" Jake asked, his brow creasing in confusion as I moved toward the desk.

Mason's expression darkened. "Nothing. Just some files."

But before I could stop myself, I opened the drawer fully, revealing a set of old photographs buried beneath a clutter of papers. The moment I laid eyes on them, a chill slithered down my spine. There, in faded black and white, was Mason's brother—smiling, vibrant, alive.

"Mason, I—"

But the words caught in my throat as I saw the shadow of a figure standing beside him, a silhouette that felt all too familiar.

The room spun, and the air grew thick with unspoken truths, leaving us teetering on the edge of a revelation that threatened to unravel everything.

Chapter 9: Shattered Masks

The rooftop is draped in the dusky glow of twilight, the city below pulsating with life, an orchestra of car horns, laughter, and distant sirens creating a chaotic symphony that both comforts and unnerves me. I lean against the cool metal railing, trying to gather my thoughts, the crisp night air tinged with the scent of street food wafting up from below. It's a strange juxtaposition—this vibrant chaos set against the churning storm inside me. I steal a glance at him, my pulse quickening, and catch a flicker of uncertainty in his gaze that makes my heart ache. He looks so at odds with the fierce persona he usually wears like armor, and for a moment, I forget the jagged edges of our history.

"Why are we here?" The question slips from my lips, softer than I intended, laced with confusion and desperation. His brows furrow, and the playfulness that often dances in his eyes gives way to something deeper—something akin to regret.

"Maybe we're here to finally stop running." His voice is low, thick with a vulnerability that makes my chest tighten. I want to believe him, to believe that we can untangle the mess we've made of each other. But as I look into his eyes, the ghosts of our past resurface, and doubt creeps in like an unwelcome guest.

"Running?" I scoff, crossing my arms defensively, feeling the familiar walls I've built around my heart start to solidify. "You've been the king of running, haven't you? Not just from me, but from everything. From what we could've been."

He takes a step closer, the city lights reflecting in his stormy gaze. "And you think you've been any better? Hiding behind your perfect little life, pretending you've moved on?" The accusation hangs between us, charged and electric. I can't help but feel a flicker of anger ignite within me, but it's quickly extinguished by the weight of truth in his words.

"Pretending?" I echo, my voice shaking slightly. "I built a life, a future I thought I wanted. It was easier than confronting the shattered pieces of my past." My heart races, the confession slipping out like a secret I hadn't meant to share. But there's something liberating in the vulnerability. I want to reach out, to mend the rift between us, but I'm terrified of the cracks that might widen with every revelation.

"Do you ever think about that night?" His question is a whisper, and it slices through the air between us, sharp and deliberate. I freeze, my stomach twisting like a tightly wound spring. That night—the night when everything fell apart, when laughter turned to tears and love was left to bleed in the shadows.

"I try not to," I admit, the weight of my words pressing down on me. "But it's always there, like a ghost haunting my steps." My voice is barely above a whisper, as if saying it too loudly might summon the memories I've buried so deeply.

"I can't forget it," he says, his tone earnest, the hurt etched into his features palpable. "Not for a single day. It's like I carry it in my bones, the weight of what we lost." He looks away, his jaw tightening, and I see the conflict warring within him—the man I knew so well at war with the man he's become.

"Why do you think we ended up here, then?" I challenge, though part of me is drawn to him, the way his vulnerability wraps around me like a warm blanket on a cold winter night. "Why do you keep coming back?"

He hesitates, running a hand through his tousled hair, the moonlight catching the glimmer of his frustration. "Maybe because I can't stand the thought of us ending like this. Not like two strangers in a city that never sleeps, two shadows of what could have been."

There's a pause, thick with unspoken words and tangled emotions. My breath catches as he takes another step closer, the space between us shrinking until it's filled with the heat radiating from our bodies. My pulse quickens, racing ahead of reason. I should push him away, put that distance back in place, but the warmth of his presence draws me in like a moth to a flame.

"Do you think we can fix this?" I ask, the question laced with a tremor of hope and fear. "Can we ever go back to what we had, or is it too late?" The words tumble out, a plea wrapped in uncertainty.

His expression shifts, vulnerability giving way to determination. "We can't go back. We can only move forward. But that doesn't mean we can't build something new." His hand brushes against mine again, electric, and I feel the walls I've built begin to crack.

"Building something new sounds daunting," I say, my voice tinged with skepticism, yet yearning. "What if we end up destroying each other all over again?"

His laughter is a soft, rich sound that warms the chill in the air. "I guess we'll just have to take the leap together and find out. I'm tired of letting fear dictate my life." His eyes are bright with a fervor that sends butterflies fluttering wildly in my stomach.

As we stand on the precipice of something profound, the city stretches out beneath us, each light a reminder of the lives and stories woven into this urban tapestry. Maybe, just maybe, amidst the chaos, we could find our own narrative again—a story filled with second chances and unexpected beginnings. And as the first stars appear, blinking down like tiny promises, I can't help but feel that perhaps this time, we might just get it right.

The weight of the night settles around us like a heavy cloak, muffling the cacophony of the city while amplifying the unspoken words lingering in the air. I feel his warmth seep into my skin, a gentle reminder that he's here, just inches away. The electricity between us crackles, as if the very air is charged with a thousand unsaid confessions. A bead of sweat drips down my temple, tracing a path across my cheek, and I brush it away with a nervous laugh, an attempt to lighten the gravity of our conversation.

"You always did have a flair for dramatic entrances," I tease, trying to recapture the playful banter that once flowed so easily between us. "Is this your new method of seduction? Whispering deep truths on rooftops while the city eavesdrops?" My tone is light, but the underlying tension remains.

He chuckles, though it sounds strained. "Well, it was either this or serenading you with a ukulele. I thought this might be less embarrassing." His eyes gleam with that familiar mischief, and for a moment, I'm transported back to lazy afternoons spent laughing over ice cream, where everything felt simple and bright.

"Trust me, you're not a ukulele kind of guy. More of a 'gritty indie rock' type," I counter, grinning. "It's probably for the best; I've seen how badly you butcher 'Wonderwall.'" The banter is a delicate dance, each word spinning around the truths we're too scared to utter.

"I'll take that as a compliment. At least I'm not the one trying to dodge emotional commitments," he replies, the playful spark in his eyes dimming slightly.

"Maybe I'm not dodging them; maybe I'm just pacing myself," I shoot back, the defensive edge creeping into my voice. I've always been good at dodging, a talent honed over years of heartbreak and disappointment. Yet, standing here with him, I feel the urge to confront what we've been avoiding. "What do you want from me?"

His expression shifts, and I can see the gears turning behind his eyes. "I want you to be honest. With me. With yourself." The sincerity in his voice tugs at something deep within me, something I've buried under layers of self-preservation.

"Honesty," I muse, the word tasting foreign on my tongue. "That's a tall order."

"Maybe we should start with baby steps. I'll go first," he suggests, taking a deep breath as if preparing to dive into the deep end. "I still think about you. A lot, actually."

His confession hangs in the air, heavy and potent, and I can almost hear the distant echo of my heart beating louder in response. "You're not the only one," I admit, the vulnerability sliding out before I can rein it in. The admission feels like stepping off a ledge, and for a moment, I teeter on the edge of that truth.

"Good," he says, relief washing over his features. "It's a start. We can't keep pretending that we don't have this... this connection."

"Connection? More like a tangled mess of emotions," I shoot back, the sharpness of my words laced with affection. "Last time I checked, feelings are messy. They don't come with a manual."

"Maybe we should write our own manual," he counters, a smile creeping back onto his face. "Step one: admit when you're terrified."

"Step two: run for the hills?" I quip, but my heart isn't in the jest. "Because that's definitely the path I'm on right now."

"Don't run, please." His tone turns earnest, eyes locking onto mine. "Let's just take a moment to breathe, okay? Right here, right now. Together."

The intensity of his gaze anchors me, and suddenly, the chaotic sounds of the city fade into the background. I want to lean into the moment, to wrap myself in the warmth of his presence, but the memories of what's been lost claw at my insides. "What if we just end up hurting each other again?" I murmur, the fear creeping back in like a shadow.

"Then at least we'll have been honest about it," he replies softly, his voice a balm to my frayed nerves. "But isn't it better to try than to sit here wondering 'what if' for the rest of our lives?"

I consider his words, weighing them against the flickering doubts that threaten to drown me. "I'm scared," I finally admit, my voice a whisper, the truth spilling out like a long-held secret. "Scared of losing you again. Scared of letting someone in."

He steps closer, bridging the gap that had felt insurmountable just moments ago. "And what if I told you that I'm terrified too? That

I'm standing here, on this rooftop, hoping we can be more than just a memory?"

There's a flicker of something in his eyes—hope, maybe? I want to reach out, to grab hold of that thread and pull it closer. "You mean it?"

"Absolutely," he replies, his gaze unwavering. "But it's going to take time. We have to be patient with each other."

"Patience has never been my strong suit," I admit, the laughter bubbling up, easing the tension.

"Then let's make a pact. We'll take it one day at a time. No expectations, just two people trying to figure it out."

I nod slowly, the prospect of taking it one step at a time feeling strangely comforting. "One day at a time, huh? That sounds manageable... and terrifying."

He grins, the mischievous glint returning. "Terrifying is just another word for exciting. And exciting is where the best stories come from."

"Are we in a story now?" I tease, but the warmth in my chest speaks of something deeper, a burgeoning hope that maybe this could be a new beginning.

"Absolutely. We're the main characters, after all. And who knows where this story will take us?"

His smile radiates like sunlight breaking through a storm, and for the first time in what feels like ages, I dare to imagine a different narrative. One filled with laughter, honesty, and the promise of a love rebuilt from the ashes of our past.

The city sprawls beneath us, a dazzling array of lights and noise, yet here on the rooftop, it feels like we exist in a bubble, a fragile sphere where reality fades away. I can still feel the warmth of his hand hovering near mine, a tantalizing reminder of what could be, yet the air is thick with tension, each moment stretched tight like a bowstring ready to snap. My heart dances between hope and fear, and I can't shake the feeling that we're teetering on the edge of something monumental.

"What if we really did take it one day at a time?" I suggest, my voice barely above a whisper. "What if we could just... start fresh?" The words taste sweet on my tongue, a bold offer wrapped in uncertainty.

"Fresh starts are overrated," he replies, a grin playing at the corners of his mouth. "But I'd settle for trying not to kill each other first."

I laugh, the sound a brief spark in the heavy air, and it feels good—too good. "I'm not sure if that's optimism or just a really low bar."

He leans against the railing, the city's glow painting shadows across his face. "Let's aim for mediocrity, then. It'll make the days easier." His casual tone belies the deeper truths swirling around us.

We fall into a comfortable silence, the hum of the city filling the gaps between our words. My heart flutters, dancing between the thrill of his presence and the weight of unresolved feelings that linger like smoke. I glance at him, the lines of his jaw illuminated by the city lights, and a sudden wave of courage washes over me.

"Do you ever think about what might have happened if we'd chosen differently? If we hadn't let everything fall apart?" The question escapes before I can stop it, and I feel my pulse quicken, anticipation and fear colliding.

His gaze drifts to the skyline, his expression turning contemplative. "All the time. It's like replaying a movie that I know by heart. I see the choices we made, the moments we let slip away."

"Which moment stands out the most?" I prod, curious and slightly anxious.

He looks at me, those stormy eyes piercing through the pretense. "The moment I left without saying goodbye. I thought I was protecting you from the mess I'd created. But in reality, I was just protecting myself."

The admission hits me hard, reverberating in the silence that follows. "I thought I was the only one who felt that way," I say softly, my voice tinged with a mixture of pain and relief. "I always wondered what I could've done differently to make you stay."

"I should have been the one fighting to stay," he admits, and for a fleeting moment, I see a glimpse of the boy I fell in love with—the one who wore his heart on his sleeve, unafraid to leap into the unknown. "But I was too afraid of what I'd become."

"Fear has a funny way of paralyzing us," I say, my voice a whisper, the truth hanging in the air like a fragile thread. "But it's also the reason we're here now, isn't it? We've both had our share of demons."

He nods, the weight of our shared history thickening the air. "What if we faced them together? What if we didn't let fear dictate our choices anymore?"

The thought is both exhilarating and terrifying. "You make it sound so simple," I reply, sarcasm edging my tone.

"Simple doesn't mean easy," he retorts, a grin breaking through. "But I'm willing to try if you are."

My heart skips, caught between disbelief and excitement. "Together?"

"Together," he affirms, and the sincerity in his voice stirs something deep within me, igniting a flicker of hope I thought long extinguished.

Suddenly, a shout from the street below shatters the moment, echoing off the buildings and pulling us back to reality. I glance down, catching sight of a crowd gathered near the entrance, their excited chatter rising up like a wave.

"What's happening?" I murmur, curiosity pulling me away from our intimate moment.

He leans over the railing, squinting down. "Looks like there's some kind of event. Probably some influencer launching a new product. You know how it is in this city."

I shake my head, a small smile breaking through. "It always seems to come back to influencers, doesn't it? I swear, if I see one more avocado toast, I might just scream."

He chuckles, but then his expression shifts, a look of concern etching into his features. "Wait, do you see that?" He points toward the crowd, and I follow his gaze.

A commotion erupts as a figure in a dark hoodie pushes through the crowd, shoving people aside with an urgency that feels out of place. My heart races, a cold shiver racing down my spine as I sense something is off.

"What's going on?" I ask, a knot forming in my stomach.

"I don't know, but—"

Before he can finish, the figure suddenly turns and sprints directly toward the hotel entrance, their movements frantic. I can feel the tension in the air thicken, like the moment before a storm breaks.

"What are they doing?" I breathe, an uneasy feeling settling over me.

"Stay here," he orders, his voice low and firm.

"Wait! No, don't—" I reach out, but he's already moving, heading toward the stairs leading down from the rooftop.

"Just stay put! I'll be right back!" he calls over his shoulder, but my instincts scream at me to follow.

As he disappears down the staircase, I'm left with the chaotic energy below and a sense of dread creeping in like a shadow. I peer over the edge again, trying to catch a glimpse of what's happening.

Suddenly, a loud crash reverberates through the air, and I see the crowd scatter, people screaming as they flee in every direction. Panic surges in my veins. "What the hell is going on?"

I grip the railing, my heart pounding as I scan the scene. A figure emerges from the chaos, looking up at the rooftop. Their eyes meet mine, and I feel my breath catch in my throat. They're not just running; they're running from something—someone.

I step back, fear curling in my stomach. And then I hear it—the unmistakable sound of sirens blaring, growing louder as they approach.

Something terrible is unfolding, and I can't shake the feeling that whatever it is, it's about to swallow us whole.

Chapter 10: The Unseen Threat

The shadows lengthen as dusk settles over the neighborhood, casting the world in hues of violet and indigo, each breath a whisper of unease that clings to me like an unwelcome scarf. I stand at the edge of my porch, the cool wood beneath my bare feet grounding me momentarily, yet the chill in the air has nothing to do with the impending winter. It's the kind of chill that seeps into your bones, a creeping dread that makes the hairs on my arms stand at attention.

My mind wanders back to the morning when I first sensed his presence, the way he had slipped between the trees in the park, his silhouette just a fleeting shadow. It was an ordinary Saturday, the sun breaking free from the clouds, illuminating the world in a golden light that felt almost cruel in hindsight. I had been sipping my coffee, relishing the rich aroma, when I noticed him. A figure lingering too long, his gaze too intense, as though I were an art piece under inspection rather than a mere passerby. I shrugged it off then, convinced it was merely my overactive imagination playing tricks on me.

But now, as the world turns dark and the comforting glow of my living room calls me in, I can't shake the feeling that he's been threading through my life ever since. I flick on the porch light, its glow piercing the deepening night, but the shadows only seem to multiply. I grab my phone, a lifeline in this tangled web of fear. The soft, familiar chime of a text message is like a lighthouse beam cutting through fog, and I welcome the distraction. It's Mia, my best friend since childhood, with her usual playful banter: "*Did you fall into a black hole? Or just your couch? Dinner soon? I'll bring dessert!*"

I smile at the message, but even her humor feels muted today. I text back, a quick response that doesn't capture the whirlpool of anxiety in my chest. "Just my couch! See you soon." As I pocket my phone, the clatter of footsteps makes me freeze. Not my imagination this time, but the unmistakable sound of someone—no, something—approaching.

My heart pounds, a wild percussion against my ribs. I peer into the shadows, straining my eyes to discern any movement, but all I see is the rustle of leaves, swayed by an unseen breeze. I step back into the house, shutting the door with a soft click that feels like a spell, warding off whatever lurks out there. Inside, the walls are adorned with photographs of laughter-filled days, my friends and family frozen in time. They seem to mock me now, their smiles impossibly bright against the murky backdrop of my thoughts.

The kettle whistles, piercing the silence, and I move to the kitchen, the familiar rhythm of routine grounding me. As I pour the steaming water into my favorite mug—its chipped edges a reminder of countless cozy evenings—I hear it again. A soft rustle, not quite a knock but a whisper against the door. My breath hitches, and for a moment, I contemplate ignoring it. After all, who could it possibly be at this hour?

Curiosity wrestles with fear as I approach the door, each step an exercise in courage. My fingers hover over the knob, and I force myself to inhale, exhaling slowly as if I could dispel the tension with my breath. When I finally open the door, it's just the night, sprawling out before me like an uninvited guest. No one is there, but the air is thick with expectation, as though it's holding its breath alongside me.

Just then, my phone buzzes again, and this time it's Mia, her message lighting up the dark screen. "Hey! I'm outside. You okay?"

Relief floods through me, and I step back into the warm glow of my home, my sanctuary. "Yeah, just thought I heard something," I text back, forcing a lightness into my words that I don't quite feel. I grab my sweater, wrapping it around me like a protective shield against the cold reality waiting outside.

As I swing the door wide, Mia stands there, a vibrant splash of color against the night, her laugh spilling over like a gentle stream.

"What were you expecting? A monster?" she teases, stepping inside and brushing the autumn leaves from her hair.

"Maybe," I reply, my voice a playful lilt, but the truth lingers, a ghost that won't leave me alone.

"Dinner's going to be amazing," she says, holding up a paper bag filled with baked goods that promise comfort. "I made your favorite."

But just as the warmth of friendship begins to envelop me, the unease returns. The air feels charged, the atmosphere thick with unsaid words, and I catch Mia's gaze flicker to the window. "You good? You seem... off," she probes, her brow furrowing slightly.

"Yeah, just a long week," I lie, the familiar tightness in my throat pushing back against my honesty.

"Uh-huh," she responds, skepticism etched into her voice. "Why don't you tell me what's really going on?"

It's easier to deflect, to pretend that everything is fine, but I can't shake the feeling that this invisible threat has woven itself into the very fabric of my life. I want to confide in Mia, to share the unease that has nestled into my bones, but how do you explain a ghost when it's invisible to everyone else?

With a sigh, I drop onto the couch, and Mia follows, her presence an anchor in the storm of my thoughts. As we dive into conversation, the laughter bubbles up between us, but the shadows outside linger, ready to whisper their secrets when the night grows too quiet. I force myself to smile, to be present, but in the back of my mind, I know he's still out there, watching, waiting.

The laughter hangs in the air like a delicate thread, weaving its way around us as Mia and I dive into a pile of warm cookies, their scent a sweet distraction from the uncertainty swirling outside. Each bite is a piece of nostalgia, a memory dipped in sugar and chocolate, and for a moment, it feels like we're children again, unburdened by the complexities of adulthood. "If you keep eating those, we'll have to roll you home," she teases, her eyes sparkling mischievously as she swipes another cookie off the plate.

"Don't tempt me," I reply, an exaggerated sigh escaping my lips. "I could absolutely get used to this new diet of cookies and more cookies."

Mia laughs, but her gaze drifts to the window, a subtle tension threading through her features. It's as if the air has shifted, pressing down on us with an unspoken weight. I follow her glance, peering into the shadows that gather just beyond the glass. The streetlights cast long fingers of light that seem to pulse, illuminating the world outside in brief flashes before the darkness swallows it whole again. "What do you see?" I ask, trying to keep my voice light, but the question hangs between us, heavy and loaded.

"Nothing. Just... the usual night things," she says, her smile faltering for a heartbeat before she shakes it off. "We should put on a movie or something. Something fluffy, to counteract the looming sense of doom."

"Fluffy sounds perfect," I agree, grateful for the distraction. Mia heads for the living room, and I follow, my heart still thrumming with an anxious rhythm. I grab the remote, flipping through the endless options, but the titles blur together, each more uninviting than the last.

"Okay, how about 'Dancing in the Rain'?" she suggests, plopping onto the couch and snatching a handful of popcorn from the bowl I'd set down. "It's practically a cure for everything."

"Sure, as long as the protagonist doesn't get stalked by some creep in the shadows," I joke, but the laughter feels brittle on my tongue. The screen flickers to life, and I sink into the couch, trying to immerse myself in the story unfolding before us.

But my mind wanders. The eerie sense of being watched returns, prickling at the back of my neck. I glance at the window again, half-expecting to see that silhouette lurking just beyond the reach of the light. It's ridiculous; it's late, and I'm safe here with Mia. Still, the creeping unease coils tighter around me.

"Earth to you," Mia calls, waving a hand in front of my face as the opening credits roll by. "I know we've got a good movie going, but you're somewhere else entirely. Spill it."

I hesitate, the words swirling in my throat. "It's just... I've been feeling a bit off lately. Like I'm being followed or something," I finally admit, my voice barely above a whisper.

Mia raises an eyebrow, her expression shifting from playful to concerned. "Followed? By whom? A shadowy figure? A ghost? Your last date?"

I can't help but chuckle at her teasing. "No, not a ghost, although that would be easier to explain. Just a guy I keep catching glimpses of around town. At the park, in the coffee shop. It feels like I'm being watched."

"Creepy. Have you thought about talking to someone? You know, like a professional? Or, I don't know, maybe a ghostbuster?" she quips, but I can see the worry etched into her features, a flicker of concern that stirs my own.

"I'm not crazy, Mia," I insist, a bit too sharply. "I can feel it, like a chill in the air when he's near. It's real."

She studies me, her brow furrowed. "Okay, I believe you. But let's not jump to conclusions. Maybe you're just stressed, or your mind is playing tricks on you."

"Yeah, because nothing screams 'I'm totally normal' like an overactive imagination," I mutter, frustration bubbling beneath the surface. "I just want to feel safe in my own life."

The movie plays on, but my thoughts drift, tangling with shadows and fears I can't quite articulate. As the protagonist dances her way through life's challenges, I find myself longing for her carefree existence, devoid of the lurking threat that has intertwined itself with my days.

After the credits roll, I shift uncomfortably on the couch, my thoughts a chaotic storm. "Let's talk about something else," I finally say, desperate to steer the conversation away from the dark shadows that have taken root in my mind.

"Fine. Let's talk about your love life—or lack thereof," Mia says, her grin returning. "Have you at least talked to that cute guy at the coffee shop?"

"I have, sort of. We exchanged smiles, and I think he knows my order by heart now," I admit, rolling my eyes playfully. "But I haven't made a move. It's hard to flirt when you feel like you're in a horror movie."

"Girl, you need to get your head in the game! He could be your distraction from all this... whatever is going on."

Her words hang in the air, an invitation to dream beyond the shadows, but I can't help but shake my head. "What if he becomes part of the problem? I mean, what if he turns out to be a shadow himself?"

"Then we'll deal with it! We'll kick his butt and have cookies in the process." She shoots me a wink, her confidence infectious.

We spend the next hour tossing around ridiculous scenarios—my coffee shop crush morphing into a rogue superhero, or a time traveler appearing in our living room with a warning of impending doom. Laughter fills the space, a balm over my growing anxiety, but as the clock ticks on, the nagging feeling in my gut resurfaces, relentless in its pursuit.

Just as Mia suggests another movie, her phone buzzes, and she glances at it, her expression shifting. "Uh, I might need to take this. It's my mom," she says, rising from the couch.

I nod, forcing a smile, but as soon as she steps away, the laughter fades, replaced by an overwhelming silence that settles like a thick fog. I take a deep breath, inhaling the scent of cookies, my heart pounding in rhythm with the echo of footsteps that only I can hear.

Alone, I allow my mind to wander back to the figure—the way he lingers in the corners of my life, always just beyond reach. What if my worries aren't mere figments of my imagination? What if they are signs, warning me of something sinister lurking beneath the surface of my otherwise ordinary existence?

The silence stretches, and I can almost hear the pulse of the night outside, a reminder that the shadows are still there, waiting, watching.

The laughter fades into the background as Mia steps outside to take her call, leaving me cocooned in the dim light of the living room. The shadows dance along the walls, teasing my imagination as they twist and stretch, and I find myself scanning the corners of the room, half-expecting to see that familiar silhouette lurking just beyond my line of sight. The familiar warmth of our earlier banter dissipates, replaced by an unsettling quiet that amplifies the echo of my thoughts.

I rise and wander to the window, peering through the glass. The street is eerily still, the only sound the rustle of leaves stirred by a soft wind. It's a deceptively peaceful scene, one that belies the growing tempest in my mind. Suddenly, I spot movement—a flicker in the shadows across the street. My heart races, adrenaline coursing through my veins. I lean closer, my breath fogging the glass, but just as quickly as it appeared, the shape vanishes into the depths of the night.

"Hey! Sorry about that," Mia says, reentering the room, her phone tucked away. "Mom wanted to know if I'm still alive."

"Did you tell her about your death-defying cookie baking skills?" I joke, hoping to mask my lingering tension, but her concerned gaze tells me she sees right through the facade.

"More like the latest drama in my life," she replies, flopping back onto the couch. "So, what's going on? You still look like you've seen a ghost."

I can't help but laugh at the irony. "I'm just being paranoid. Nothing to worry about."

Mia's eyes narrow, her expression skeptical. "You're not fooling me. Spill it."

"I swear, it's just—" The words catch in my throat. What if I told her the truth? That there's something about this stranger, this unseen threat, that claws at the back of my mind, making it impossible to focus on anything else? Instead, I deflect, "It's just been a long week, you know?"

"Long weeks are for catching up on Netflix and eating entire bags of popcorn. Not for worrying about imaginary monsters."

"Touché," I concede, but the laughter fades as quickly as it comes. The weight of my fears presses heavily against my chest. I can't shake the feeling that this isn't just an overactive imagination at play.

Mia glances at her watch, then back at me. "How about we switch gears? Let's find something ridiculous to watch. I'm pretty sure my mom still has that old VHS of 'Dance Off in the Valley.' You remember that gem, right?"

"Of course! I still can't believe we thought that was a masterpiece," I say, the memory igniting a spark of joy amid the fog of anxiety.

We dig through the clutter in the living room, and Mia emerges triumphantly, holding the dusty VHS like it's a trophy. "I can't believe we actually used to watch this," she laughs, "but hey, it's the perfect distraction."

As the movie whirls into life, we lose ourselves in the antics of characters who seem both outlandish and strangely relatable. Yet, no matter how hard I try to immerse myself in the frivolity, a nagging sensation gnaws at me. With each scene, I can't help but glance toward the window, half-expecting the figure to reappear.

Mia chats animatedly about her latest crush while I nod along, but I'm only half-listening. My thoughts drift back to the unsettling feeling of being watched. The laughter on-screen fades into a distant murmur, and I'm pulled into a spiraling abyss of paranoia.

Suddenly, a loud crash from outside jolts me back to reality. My heart leaps into my throat, and I bolt upright, adrenaline spiking through me. "What was that?"

"Probably just a raccoon or something," Mia says, but her voice trembles slightly, betraying her own unease.

"Right. Because raccoons are known for crashing parties at midnight," I reply, trying to keep my tone light. But the truth is, the idea of a raccoon is far more comforting than the prospect of facing whatever might be lurking outside.

"Should we check it out?" Mia suggests, glancing toward the window, a mixture of curiosity and fear in her eyes.

"Are we really going to play that game? I mean, we've seen enough horror movies to know how this ends." I tease, but inside, I'm spiraling.

"We can't just ignore it. What if someone needs help?"

Against my better judgment, I nod. "Fine. But if we get chased by a maniac, I'm blaming you."

"Deal!" she replies, a brave smile illuminating her face despite the tension hanging in the air.

We approach the window, our breaths synchronized as we peer into the darkness. The street is still, but the feeling of something being off swells like a tide. I shiver, the warmth of the room suddenly feeling distant.

As we step outside, the chill wraps around us like a heavy blanket, and the world feels more expansive than it did indoors. The light from the porch casts a halo on the ground, but beyond that, the shadows loom, thick and oppressive.

"Maybe it was just a branch or something," I whisper, hoping to quell the rising anxiety in my chest.

"Or it could be the world's most determined raccoon," Mia replies, scanning the darkness with a wary eye.

We venture further, our footsteps muffled against the damp grass, and I can't shake the sense of being pulled into a trap. The neighborhood, usually alive with the distant sounds of cars and laughter, is now deathly silent.

"Okay, this is officially creepy," I mutter, glancing over my shoulder. "I swear, if I see someone hiding in the bushes, I'm going to scream."

Just then, I catch a glimpse of movement out of the corner of my eye—a figure darting between the trees at the edge of the yard. My heart races, and I grab Mia's arm. "Did you see that?"

"See what?" she asks, her voice rising with panic as she searches the dark with wide eyes.

"There! Right over there!" I point, my breath hitching. But as I strain to focus, the figure dissolves into the shadows, leaving nothing but the rustling leaves and my racing heartbeat echoing in the stillness.

"Maybe we should go back inside?" Mia suggests, her voice trembling slightly.

Before I can respond, the sound of footsteps—heavy and deliberate—echoes through the darkness. My blood runs cold as I realize it's not just a trick of the night. Someone is approaching, and this time, it's not my imagination.

"Run!" I shout, grabbing Mia's hand, and together we sprint back toward the safety of the porch, the world behind us dissolving into chaos. As we reach the door, I fumble for the handle, my heart pounding like a drum in my chest. But the door won't budge.

Panic surges through me, and I whirl around just as the figure steps into the light, his features obscured but the menace in his posture unmistakable. "You shouldn't have come outside," he says, his voice smooth and chilling, an echo of everything I had feared.

The world tilts on its axis as dread fills every fiber of my being, and in that moment, I know this is only the beginning.

Chapter 11: Echoes of Secrets

I sift through his belongings with the reverence of an archaeologist, each item revealing layers of a man I thought I knew intimately. The familiar scent of cedar and sandalwood hangs in the air, mingling with the faint traces of his cologne—an olfactory reminder of the warmth of his embrace. Sunlight streams through the sheer curtains, casting soft patterns on the wooden floor, illuminating forgotten memories wrapped in dust. I feel like an intruder in this sacred space, trespassing on the sanctity of our shared moments, but the insistent pulse of suspicion drives me deeper into the labyrinth of his life.

His desk is cluttered with papers—bills, notes, and what appears to be sketches of our life together, lovingly annotated in his precise handwriting. Each line holds a piece of his heart, but what gnaws at me are the scattered notes that flicker like distant stars, hinting at secrets I'm not meant to see. I shove aside a couple of magazines, their covers featuring headlines that sing of romance and intrigue, like a chorus to my disquiet. Among the chaos lies a small wooden box, intricately carved, its surface polished to a sheen. It feels deceptively innocent, yet my intuition screams for me to look closer.

With trembling fingers, I lift the lid. Inside, a collection of photographs spills out—moments captured in time, laughter frozen in place. There's one of us at the beach, the sun dipping low on the horizon, painting the sky in shades of pink and orange, our fingers intertwined like roots growing deeper into the earth. I linger on that image, nostalgia tugging at my heart, before I shuffle through the rest. The smiles are infectious, yet I notice something odd in the background of one—an unfamiliar figure, partially obscured, a shadow lurking just out of reach. My breath hitches as I realize this isn't just a scrapbook of our love; it's a gallery of our secrets.

The notebook beneath the floorboards beckons to me like a siren's call, and despite the unease tightening in my chest, I can't resist its pull.

I pry it loose, dust motes swirling in the air like the remnants of lost dreams, and settle into his worn armchair, a space that smells of him, but now feels like an alien planet. I crack open the cover, the spine creaking like a door to another world, revealing scrawls that range from meticulous observations to frantic jottings, a mosaic of his thoughts laid bare.

As I read, my heart plummets. It isn't just about me; it's about all of us. Names leap off the pages like specters from a past I thought we'd left behind. Some I recognize from hushed conversations, like echoes of laughter fading into the night, and others are strangers—mysteries he has entwined in our lives like a spider's web. Each entry is laced with an urgency that chills me, as if he's been preparing for something monumental, a reckoning I'm not yet ready to face.

"Who the hell is Vivian Greene?" I whisper to myself, the name a bitter taste in my mouth. I flip the page frantically, scouring for answers. Notes follow, cryptic and charged: "Contact on the brink of a breakthrough," "Caution advised," "Family ties stronger than blood." My mind races, weaving connections I never wanted to acknowledge. My chest tightens as I read about dinners held in secret, late-night meetings shrouded in shadows, and discussions that hinted at darker undertones I had blithely overlooked in the comfort of our routine.

"Damn it, Jake," I mutter, the air thick with disbelief and betrayal. Each revelation feels like a knife twisting in my gut. This man, who had painted our life in vibrant colors, is now an enigma wrapped in layers of deceit. I thought I knew him—every quirk, every glance—but what else lies hidden beneath that familiar facade?

A sudden noise jolts me from my spiraling thoughts, the sound of keys rattling in the door. My heart leaps into my throat as I scramble to close the notebook, panic electrifying my movements. I hastily shove it back beneath the floorboards, but I can't erase the unease that lingers in the air like a thick fog. I collapse back into the armchair, attempting to steady my breathing as the door swings open.

Jake steps inside, a gust of autumn air trailing behind him, tousling his hair in a way that once struck me as charming. But now, it feels like a betrayal—a reminder of the comfort I thought we shared, now tainted by shadows lurking in the corners. He flashes a smile, and for a fleeting moment, my heart leaps. But then I remember the secrets he keeps, the lives entwined with ours like a jigsaw puzzle missing key pieces.

"Hey, you!" he exclaims, shedding his jacket with a casual ease that masks the storm brewing beneath my surface. "I thought I'd surprise you with dinner." He moves to the kitchen, humming an off-key tune, blissfully unaware of the tempest brewing within me.

"Dinner sounds great," I manage, the words sticking to my throat like dry sand. Each syllable feels like a lie, a masquerade ball where I wear the mask of the unsuspecting girlfriend while my insides churn with the revelations I've unearthed.

As he busies himself with pans and spices, I wrestle with the urge to confront him, to unravel the web of deceit before me. But as I watch him, laughter lines crinkling around his eyes, a pang of longing pierces through the tumult. I don't want to lose this man I love, even as I realize I might not know him at all.

"Everything okay?" he asks, glancing back at me, a hint of concern knitting his brow.

I nod, forcing a smile that feels like it might crack. "Just a little tired," I lie, the weight of the truth hanging heavily in the air between us.

He returns to his cooking, blissfully unaware, and I wonder how many more secrets lie beneath this surface, hidden just out of reach, waiting for the moment I dare to pull them into the light. As the aroma of garlic and herbs fills the kitchen, the warmth of home wraps around me like a soft blanket, yet the chill of uncertainty creeps in, reminding me that sometimes, love isn't as simple as it seems.

The scent of sautéed garlic wafts through the air, mingling with the uneasy knot in my stomach as Jake stirs a bubbling pot of something that looks suspiciously like a culinary masterpiece. His laughter echoes softly, a melody that dances around the kitchen, but I can hardly hear it over the sound of my own racing thoughts. I want to believe that the warmth radiating from him can melt away the chill of doubt that has seeped into my bones. But the shadows of the notebook and the cryptic names linger in my mind, a cacophony of questions begging for answers I'm not yet ready to confront.

"Are you going to help, or just sit there looking suspicious?" he teases, glancing over his shoulder, his playful tone cutting through my reverie like a knife.

"I'm just... absorbing your culinary genius," I reply, trying to infuse a lightness into my voice that feels foreign. My smile feels tight, more a mask than a genuine expression, and I can't shake the way his gaze lingers, as if he's waiting for something more.

"Absorbing? You're not the only one who's hungry, you know," he retorts, his playful smirk igniting a spark of warmth. It's moments like this—when his eyes light up with mischief—that I remind myself of the man I fell for, the one whose laughter felt like a refuge from the storm. "Come on, chop these vegetables while I finish up."

With a huff that's half annoyance, half affection, I saunter over to the counter. As I grab a knife, the cool steel against my palm reminds me of the warmth of our relationship, yet it feels more like a weapon now, one I could wield against the secrets that threaten to slice through our bond. I start chopping with mechanical precision, my mind wandering back to the notebook and the implications of what I read. What had he uncovered about us that I didn't know?

The sound of knife against cutting board fills the silence, a rhythm that barely masks the tension thrumming beneath the surface. I steal glances at Jake as he stirs and seasonings float up, fragrant and inviting, yet I can't help but feel they're tainted by the revelations I've unearthed.

"Hey," he interrupts my spiral, placing a gentle hand on my wrist, grounding me. "What's going on in that beautiful mind of yours? You look like you're trying to solve a mystery, and I'm not talking about dinner."

I feign a laugh, the sound brittle in the warm kitchen. "Just thinking about how to keep you from burning the house down," I quip, my tone light yet forced. The worry flickering in his eyes pulls at my heartstrings, and I realize I can't keep pretending.

"I'm fine, really," I say, the words spilling out in a rush. "Just... tired from work, you know? It's been a long week."

He studies me, his brow furrowing as if he can see through my facade. "You know you can talk to me, right? About anything?" His voice is low, sincere, the way it used to be when we first started dating, before the shadows of doubt crept in.

I nod, swallowing hard against the lump in my throat. "Yeah, I know." I want to tell him everything—the notebook, the names, the secrets that ripple through the fabric of our lives—but the words hang heavy on my tongue, tangled in a web of fear and uncertainty. What if he doesn't see me the same way afterward? What if I shatter the fragile illusion of our perfect world?

The meal progresses, and as we settle at the table, the warmth of the food and the intimacy of the moment wrap around us. I take a bite, the flavors exploding on my tongue, but the taste is bittersweet, each morsel flavored by my unspoken doubts.

"So, what's the latest with that project of yours?" he asks, the casual tone of his voice a soothing balm, yet I can't help but notice the way his eyes flicker with a hint of distraction, as if he's mentally sifting through his own secrets.

I share a little about work, details about a client that I know he'll find interesting. "We're finally getting the hang of this new software implementation," I say, hoping to lure him into the flow of our usual banter, where we dissect our day like a pair of seasoned detectives.

"That's great! I knew you'd whip them into shape," he replies, a proud smile lighting up his face, momentarily distracting me from my inner turmoil.

"Let's just hope they don't come to me crying when the next deadline hits," I joke, and the air around us lightens, momentarily lifting the weight of the secrets hanging in the periphery.

But as the conversation flows, my mind keeps wandering back to the notebook and the specter of Vivian Greene. The name dances on my tongue, a specter I can't shake. "What's the deal with Vivian?" I blurt out, before I can catch myself.

Jake freezes, his fork pausing mid-air, and in that split second, I see the flicker of something—fear? Guilt? I can't quite place it, but it twists in my gut like a coiled serpent. "Vivian?" he echoes, the name sliding from his lips like ice.

"Yeah, I found her name in some of your notes," I say, keeping my voice even, though my heart races in anticipation. "Who is she?"

He places his fork down, leaning back in his chair, a shift in his demeanor that sends alarm bells ringing in my head. "You shouldn't have gone through my things, Amelia."

His tone, typically playful, is now laced with a sternness that makes my breath hitch. "I was just... curious," I manage, though I know it sounds weak, like an excuse. "You've been acting strange lately, and I thought maybe—"

"Maybe you should trust me instead of rummaging through my life like some detective on a soap opera," he interjects, the frustration in his voice sharp enough to slice through the tension like a knife.

"I'm not a detective, Jake, but you're hiding things! You can't expect me to ignore it when your life is literally written down in that notebook!" The words tumble out before I can stop them, fueled by a mix of anger and desperation.

The silence stretches between us, thick and palpable. His expression shifts from frustration to something unreadable, and my heart sinks as I realize I've opened a door I might not be able to close.

"Amelia," he starts, his voice softening, and I brace myself for what comes next. "There are things I haven't told you—things that I'm not proud of. But it's not because I don't care about you. I do."

"Then tell me!" I urge, my voice rising, the kitchen suddenly feeling too small, the walls closing in around me. "If you really care, then why keep me in the dark?"

He leans forward, his eyes narrowing, searching my face for something I can't define. "Because sometimes the truth is complicated. And sometimes, it's better to keep certain things buried."

"Better for whom?" I fire back, my heart pounding in my chest. The air between us crackles with tension, each word stinging like a fresh wound.

He opens his mouth, hesitating, and for a moment, I think he might finally spill the secrets that have haunted him. But then he closes it again, the moment slipping through our fingers like sand.

"I can't do this right now," he finally says, his voice tight, a wall sliding into place.

I feel a chill wash over me, the warmth of the dinner fading into an uncomfortable chill. "So, we're just going to pretend everything's fine?"

His gaze hardens, and the moment stretches like taut wire. "I need time," he replies finally, the weight of those words crashing down on us like a storm cloud.

Time. The word echoes in my mind, a reminder of the distance that now stretches between us. As he turns back to his plate, the silence falls heavier than before, leaving me stranded on the precipice of secrets that threaten to pull us apart. The clinking of cutlery now feels like the distant sound of a clock ticking, counting down to an uncertain future I can't bear to imagine.

The silence between us stretches taut as a drawn bowstring, every unspoken word charged with the weight of revelations left unsaid. I can feel the atmosphere shifting, a storm brewing beneath the surface of our carefully curated dinner. Jake's eyes flicker, a combination of apprehension and something deeper—fear, perhaps, or guilt. It's unsettling, like watching a shadow dance just beyond the light.

"Look, I didn't mean to go through your things," I say, my voice steady despite the tremor in my hands. "But when you started pulling away, I had to know what was going on."

"Pulling away?" He echoes my words like a mantra, a wall of defense rising between us. "That's a bit dramatic, don't you think?"

"Dramatic? It's not like I've imagined the coldness in our conversations or the way you've been dodging my questions," I fire back, frustration bubbling over. "You think I enjoy feeling like a stranger in my own home?"

He stares at me, the lines of his jaw tightening. "You're right. I have been distant. But digging into my life won't fix anything, Amelia."

"Then what will?" The question bursts from my lips before I can filter it. The desperation hanging in the air feels almost tangible, like a thick fog wrapping around us, muffling the warmth that once filled our shared moments.

Jake leans back, his gaze flicking away as if searching for an answer in the dimly lit corners of the kitchen. "You wouldn't understand," he says finally, his tone a mix of sadness and resolve.

"Try me," I insist, leaning forward, a fierce determination bubbling inside me. "I want to understand. I want to help."

"Sometimes the things we want to protect are better off hidden," he murmurs, and in that moment, the air thickens with unspoken truths. The shadows of his past loom large between us, and I can't shake the feeling that whatever he's guarding is a volatile secret, one that might shatter everything we've built together.

The dinner plates feel like weights anchoring us down, the food now cold and unappetizing. I push mine away, suddenly losing my appetite. "You're pushing me away, Jake. And I can't just stand by while you drown in whatever this is," I say, my voice cracking under the strain of my emotions.

He looks at me, really looks at me, and for a moment, the facade of indifference crumbles. "It's not about you, Amelia. It's about the choices I've made—things I've done."

"What things?" My heart races as a hundred scenarios play out in my mind, each more frightening than the last. "Is this about Vivian? Who is she, really?"

The kitchen feels suddenly smaller, the walls closing in, suffocating. Jake stands, pushing his chair back with a scrape that sounds like nails on a chalkboard. "You need to stop this," he says, his voice low and dangerous. "You have no idea what you're asking for."

"Then enlighten me!" I rise, matching his intensity, feeling the anger pulse through me like a second heartbeat. "If you care about me at all, you'll tell me the truth."

He runs a hand through his hair, frustration etched in every line of his face. "You're not ready for the truth, Amelia. I promise you, it'll change everything."

"Try me," I challenge again, my heart pounding in my chest like a drum heralding a coming storm. "I can handle it."

The moment hangs between us, heavy with unfulfilled desires and regret. I can see him weighing the options, the pull of secrecy versus the lure of honesty, and my stomach churns with the uncertainty of it all.

"Okay," he finally concedes, his voice barely above a whisper. "But you need to understand—once you know, there's no going back."

"Just tell me!" I urge, stepping closer, desperate for him to take that leap into vulnerability.

He swallows hard, his gaze slipping to the floor as if he's trying to draw courage from the wood grain. "Vivian... she's not just someone from my past. She's involved in something dangerous—something I got wrapped up in before I met you."

A chill washes over me, seeping through my skin and settling into my bones. "What do you mean, 'involved in something dangerous'?"

He hesitates, his eyes darkening with a mixture of regret and something like fear. "There are people involved in this—people I owe money to, people I've made promises to. And Vivian... she's the connection. She's the one who got me into it."

"Got you into what?" The question feels like a stone lodged in my throat, my heart racing as I sense the magnitude of what he's saying.

"A smuggling operation," he admits, each word slicing through the air with lethal precision. "I was young and stupid. I thought I could handle it. But I couldn't. And now... now it's come back to haunt me."

The revelation hits me like a tidal wave, crashing over my carefully constructed world. "Smuggling? You were involved in that?" I can hardly process it, my mind racing to grasp the implications. "And you didn't think to tell me?"

"Because I didn't want you to be dragged into it!" he explodes, the pent-up frustration spilling over. "I was trying to protect you!"

"By lying to me? By hiding who you really are?" I shake my head, disbelief swirling in my chest. "How could you think that would keep me safe?"

His eyes flash with pain, and in that moment, I see the battle raging within him. "I thought I could leave it behind, that it was all over. But Vivian has resurfaced, and so have the people I thought I'd escaped."

"Resurfaced? What does that mean?" The pit in my stomach deepens, my heart racing at the thought of what might be coming.

"There's been a threat," he admits, his voice now hoarse. "They've come looking for me. I don't know how they found me, but it's not over, Amelia. They want what I owe, and they won't stop until they get it."

Panic rises in my throat, and I struggle to catch my breath. "What are we supposed to do?" I ask, my voice trembling. "Are we in danger?"

"I'll protect you," he promises, but the way his eyes dart around the room tells me he's not so sure.

Just then, a loud bang echoes from the front of the apartment—sharp and jarring, like a gunshot ringing through the air. My heart races as I freeze, dread pooling in my stomach.

"What was that?" I whisper, barely able to form the words.

Jake's expression shifts, the realization dawning on him as he stares at the door, a storm brewing in his eyes. "Stay here," he orders, urgency threading through his voice.

"No, I'm coming with you!" I protest, adrenaline coursing through my veins, pushing me to move, to take action.

But he grabs my arm, his grip firm and resolute. "You have to trust me. I'll handle this."

The tension crackles like electricity, and I can see the determination in his eyes—he's made up his mind. I want to scream at him, to make him understand that this isn't just his fight; it's ours.

Another bang resonates through the apartment, this one louder, more insistent. The walls seem to tremble with the force of it, and my pulse quickens, every instinct screaming at me to run.

"Jake!" I call out, but he's already moving, his footsteps echoing against the hardwood floor as he strides toward the door.

"Lock the bedroom door and don't come out!" he shouts back, but his voice is swallowed by the chaos that's unfolding just outside.

Fear grips me like a vice, and I dart toward the bedroom, each step a battle against the urge to turn back, to confront him about the choices he's making. But I can't linger, can't ignore the pounding urgency in my chest that tells me something terrible is about to happen.

I reach the bedroom and slam the door behind me, locking it with shaking hands. The sound of shouting echoes through the apartment, distorted and frantic, and I press my ear against the door, straining to hear what's happening.

"Don't! Get away from me!" Jake's voice cuts through the chaos, raw and desperate.

My heart races, a wild animal in a cage, desperate to break free. I want to help him, but I can't open that door. The fear that has taken root in my chest grows, a gnawing certainty that whatever is happening out there is about to change everything between us.

Then, silence. The kind that blankets everything, heavy and foreboding. My breath hitches as I step back from the door, dread pooling in the pit of my stomach. What if he's in trouble? What if I've just locked him out in a moment of danger?

And just as I turn to look for another way out, a slow, deliberate creaking fills the air—the sound of the door handle turning. My heart plummets as I freeze in place, every instinct screaming at me to run. But there's nowhere to go.

The door swings open, revealing a shadowy figure standing in the threshold, a chilling grin spreading across their face.

Chapter 12: Midnight Revelation

The moon hung low in the sky, a gleaming sentinel illuminating the empty pier where the scent of brine mingled with the crispness of the autumn air. I could hear the gentle lapping of water against the worn wooden posts, a rhythmic heartbeat echoing my own escalating pulse. It was a night that felt charged, electric, as if the very universe was holding its breath, waiting for the storm that loomed on the horizon—both in the sky and in my heart.

Standing there, I faced him. The man who had been my ally, my source of hope, and now, my greatest enigma. His silhouette was sharp against the silvery backdrop, the flickering lights from the distant shore casting an ethereal glow on his face. There was an intensity in his gaze that unsettled me; it was as if he held the secrets of the world, and I was but a curious child trying to unravel them. My breath caught in my throat as I prepared to unleash the accusations that had been brewing within me, stewing like a pot left unattended on the stove.

"You lied to me," I said, the words slicing through the stillness like a knife through flesh. The accusation hung in the air, taut and unresolved, vibrating with the weight of betrayal. I could see a flicker of something in his eyes—shame, perhaps? Regret? Or was it simply the reflection of the moonlight, betraying no more than the currents beneath the surface?

"I never meant to," he replied, his voice low and gravelly, each syllable dripping with sincerity. It felt like a lifeline thrown into turbulent waters, but I was too busy treading the chaos of my emotions to grab hold. "You think you're the only one running?" His question pierced the veil of my anger, drawing me closer to the truth I had refused to acknowledge.

I folded my arms, my heart racing as I took a step back, the sound of my boots thudding against the planks felt overly loud in the silence that enveloped us. "Running? From what? From you?" I laughed, a bitter sound that hung heavy in the night. "You're the one who dragged me into this mess. All those secrets, all those lies."

He took a step forward, his eyes locked onto mine, and I could feel the heat radiating off him like an open flame. "It's not that simple, and you know it." His voice deepened, resonating with a raw intensity that made my heart falter. "There are things you don't understand—things I can't explain."

"Try me," I challenged, though a tremor of fear crept into my voice. I had always thought of myself as brave, resilient in the face of adversity. Yet here I was, trembling under the weight of his truth. The shadows of the past wrapped around us like a shroud, each revelation threatening to suffocate me.

He hesitated, the tension between us thick enough to slice through. "You think this is just about us?" His words were sharp, each one laden with unshed memories. "There are forces at play here far more dangerous than either of us."

I could see the shadows of his past reflected in his eyes, the battles fought and lost, the burdens carried in silence. I had wanted to see him as the villain, but as he spoke, I began to understand the depth of his struggle. The lines of his face were etched with pain, every crease telling a story of sacrifice and choices made in darkness.

"Then tell me," I urged, my voice barely a whisper. "Tell me why you've been running. Why you brought me into this world of chaos."

The moonlight cast a silver veil over him, softening the harsh angles of his features. "Because I thought I could protect you," he admitted, his vulnerability disarming me. "But I was wrong. This isn't just about me; it's about a game that's been played long before we met. We're pawns, both of us, caught in a web of deceit that stretches far beyond this moment."

A chill ran down my spine as the realization hit me. "You mean to say that we're just... players? In someone else's game?" My voice trembled with disbelief. "You put my life at risk for a game?"

His expression hardened for a moment, a flicker of anger flashing across his face. "It's not just a game. It's survival. If we don't play our parts, we won't survive the fallout."

I searched his gaze, searching for the truth buried beneath the layers of pain and complexity. "What does that mean? What do you want from me?"

"I want you to understand," he said, his tone softening. "I want you to see that I'm not the enemy you think I am. I'm fighting to keep you safe, even if it means walking through fire to do it."

My heart twisted in my chest, a maelstrom of emotions surging within me. "And what about the trust we built? You shattered that the moment you chose silence over honesty."

"I had my reasons," he countered, his voice tinged with desperation. "But now it's too late for second chances. The storm is coming, and we need to prepare."

"Prepare for what?" I asked, dread coiling in my stomach.

"For the truth," he replied, the weight of those words hanging heavy in the air. "And the consequences of our choices. This night may not end how we want it to."

As I stood there, the cool breeze ruffled my hair, the scent of saltwater mingling with the promise of impending danger. My world felt unsteady, the ground shifting beneath me like the restless waves crashing against the pier. Yet amidst the uncertainty, I could sense the resolve in his presence, a fierce determination that ignited a flicker of hope within me.

With each passing moment, I realized that the man I thought I knew was as layered and complex as the world we found ourselves in. We were both seeking something—answers, safety, perhaps even redemption in a world that thrived on shadows and whispers. And as the moon climbed higher, illuminating the path ahead, I knew that whatever came next, we would face it together, two reluctant heroes tangled in a fate we had yet to fully comprehend.

The tension hung thick between us, a taut line stretched to its breaking point. I could feel the chill of the night seeping into my bones, mingling with the heat radiating from him. It was as if the very air conspired to keep us entangled in this dance of accusations and revelations. I had stepped onto this pier believing I held the upper hand, that I could corner him with my truths. But now, faced with the vulnerability etched into his features, I felt the ground shift beneath my feet once more.

"I didn't ask for this," I blurted, the frustration spilling out like water from a cracked dam. "I didn't ask for you to drag me into your twisted world of secrets."

"Twisted?" He raised an eyebrow, a hint of amusement playing at the corners of his mouth, though his eyes remained serious. "You think this is a game to me? You think I enjoy the shadows?"

"You seem pretty cozy in them," I shot back, crossing my arms defensively. The wind picked up, whipping my hair around my face, and I brushed it away impatiently. "You've made your choices, and I'm just supposed to accept them because you've decided I'm a player now?"

"Whether you accept it or not doesn't change the facts." He took a step closer, the space between us pulsing with unspoken truths. "We're both in this deep, whether you want to acknowledge it. The world isn't as black and white as we'd like it to be."

I took a deep breath, steeling myself against the encroaching doubts. "So what's next? We embrace the chaos and hope for the best?"

He ran a hand through his hair, frustration evident in the way he clenched his jaw. "No. We strategize. We fight back against whatever is coming for us." His gaze hardened, determination burning bright in his expression. "You're not just a pawn, and neither am I. We're more than that, even if we don't feel it right now."

"Right, because that's reassuring." I laughed dryly, the sound mingling with the distant call of a seagull, a fitting backdrop for my sardonic mood. "And what happens when the game turns deadly?"

"Then we play to win." There was a fierceness in his tone that sent a shiver down my spine, a glimmer of the man I had once trusted—the one who had inspired me to believe that we could overcome anything together.

Before I could respond, the night erupted into chaos. A sharp crack pierced the air, followed by a blinding flash that illuminated the darkened sky. I flinched instinctively, ducking as a bright light burst from the direction of the city, the distant sounds of sirens echoing in the distance. "What was that?" Panic surged through me, my heart racing as adrenaline flooded my veins.

"Trouble," he replied tersely, his eyes narrowing as he scanned the horizon. "We need to move. Now."

"Move? You're not even going to explain what's happening?" I shot back, incredulity lacing my voice. "I thought we were having a moment here."

"A moment? We'll have our moments later—if we survive this." He stepped forward, grasping my arm with a firm but gentle grip, pulling me back from the edge of the pier. "Trust me, please."

Trust. The word hung heavy in the air, weighed down by the memories of his secrets. But as the chaos erupted around us, I found myself nodding, a reluctant acceptance taking hold. "Fine. But you owe me an explanation."

As we raced down the pier, the once tranquil scene transformed into a whirlwind of uncertainty. The air felt electric, charged with impending danger. The moon, a silent observer, cast long shadows that danced at our feet as we sprinted toward the safety of the shore.

"We're being watched," he muttered, glancing back over his shoulder. "I'm not sure how much time we have, but whoever is behind this won't stop until they find us."

"Find us? Why would they be looking for you? You're just a—"

"A pawn in a bigger game, I know," he interrupted, urgency creeping into his voice. "But there are pieces on this board that won't hesitate to eliminate anyone who threatens their plans."

My heart raced in my chest, the truth of his words sending a fresh wave of fear coursing through me. "And what exactly does that mean for us?"

"It means we need to blend in, disappear until we figure out our next move." He pulled me toward a narrow alley that cut through the bustling streets. The sounds of the pier faded behind us, replaced by the cacophony of the city. The vibrant neon lights flickered overhead, casting strange shadows that danced around us, blurring the line between reality and something more sinister.

"Disappearing isn't exactly my specialty," I replied, trying to lighten the moment, but the tremor in my voice betrayed me. "I'm more of a 'stand and fight' kind of girl."

"Then we'll stand and fight," he promised, his grip tightening around my hand as we slipped into the alley. "But first, we need to think. They won't expect us to take the fight to them."

We reached a hidden corner where the din of the street was muted, and he leaned against the cool brick wall, his breath coming in quick bursts. "We need to figure out who is after us and why."

"Great plan," I said, trying to catch my breath as I leaned beside him, the warmth of his body igniting a sense of familiarity in the midst of chaos. "But do you even know where to start?"

"I have a few ideas." He ran a hand through his hair, frustration evident in his furrowed brow. "I know a contact—someone who can provide information. But we need to be cautious. We can't trust anyone right now."

"Anyone?" I raised an eyebrow, skepticism coloring my tone. "You just told me you'd do anything to keep me safe, and now I'm supposed to question everyone we encounter? This is starting to feel a little paranoid, don't you think?"

"Paranoid is how you stay alive," he countered, his voice steady but his eyes betraying the flicker of uncertainty beneath the bravado. "It's not about mistrust; it's about survival."

"Survival, right. So, what's the plan?" I asked, a mixture of frustration and excitement bubbling beneath the surface.

"First, we get somewhere safe and assess our options. After that, we contact my informant. But you need to promise me one thing."

"What's that?" I shifted my weight, intrigued by the serious tone that had returned to his voice.

"Promise me that no matter what you hear, you'll stay by my side. We're in this together, remember?"

His words wrapped around me like a lifeline, and I could feel the weight of his sincerity. "Okay, I promise," I said, and for the first time that night, I meant it.

Together, we stood at the precipice of uncertainty, poised on the brink of discovery and danger. As the city continued its vibrant dance around us, I could feel the pull of fate drawing us deeper into a world woven with shadows and light, trust and treachery.

The alley swallowed us whole, the cacophony of the city muffled to a distant hum, replaced by the oppressive weight of uncertainty. As I leaned against the cool brick wall, I could hear the rush of my heartbeat echoing in the silence. The streetlights cast a soft glow, illuminating our faces and highlighting the tension that hummed in the air between us.

"Okay, then, what's the game plan?" I asked, my voice steadying as determination settled into my bones. "You said you know someone who can help us. Who are they?"

He glanced around, his eyes sharp and assessing, as if he were a hawk surveying the landscape for any signs of danger. "Her name is Lila. She runs a bar downtown, a dive where the shadows are as thick as the smoke. She's got connections, and she can help us navigate this mess."

"Sounds charming," I remarked, a hint of sarcasm slipping into my tone. "Do I get to order a drink while we're at it, or is this strictly business?"

"Definitely business," he replied, the corners of his mouth twitching into a smirk. "But I can't promise we won't end up sharing a drink. It's practically tradition in her place."

I rolled my eyes, but the flicker of amusement lightened the air just a bit. "So, where's this magical dive?"

"Just a few blocks from here," he said, taking my hand again, this time with a sense of urgency. "Follow me, and whatever you do, don't look back."

With that, we stepped out of the alley, our hearts racing in sync as we maneuvered through the thrumming heart of the city. The streets were alive, the hum of laughter and music spilling from nearby venues like an enticing perfume. It felt surreal, navigating through the vibrant chaos while shadows loomed just behind us.

As we approached the bar, its neon sign flickered above the entrance, casting a kaleidoscope of colors onto the cracked pavement. The place had an unkempt charm, with a battered jukebox cranking out tunes that seemed both timeless and out of place. The door creaked ominously as we entered, the scent of stale beer and something sweetly pungent hitting me like a wave.

Inside, the atmosphere was thick with smoke and secrets. Dimly lit tables dotted the room, and patrons leaned into hushed conversations, their faces obscured by shadows. I followed him through the crowd, my pulse quickening with every step. This was a place where stories were woven, lives intersected, and trouble lurked in every corner.

"There she is," he said, nodding toward a woman sitting at the far end of the bar. Lila was striking, with a cascade of fiery red hair and eyes that gleamed with mischief and knowledge. She wore a leather jacket that had seen better days but clung to her like armor.

"Lila!" he called out, weaving through the throng. She turned, her expression shifting from boredom to intrigue in an instant as she spotted him.

"Look who's back from the dead," she quipped, her voice smooth like the whiskey she poured for herself. "And you've brought a friend. Care to introduce her, or are we keeping this one a secret?"

"This is... a very important friend," he replied, his tone serious now. "We need your help."

She raised an eyebrow, scrutinizing me with an intensity that made me feel exposed. "Important enough to attract trouble?"

"Trouble's got a way of finding us," I muttered, crossing my arms as I leaned against the bar. "What can you do?"

Lila leaned back, swirling the amber liquid in her glass. "Depends on what you need. But if it involves getting rid of a few unwanted guests, I might know a thing or two about that."

"Unwanted guests?" I repeated, anxiety creeping back into my voice. "What exactly are we talking about?"

"Let's just say," she began, her tone turning conspiratorial, "that there are eyes everywhere, and they've been looking for him. And now you're on their radar too."

My heart sank as the reality of our situation crashed over me. "What do you mean by 'eyes everywhere'?"

Lila leaned forward, her voice dropping to a whisper. "You're caught in a web, sweetheart. This isn't just about your friend's past; it's about what he represents—something much bigger than either of you realized."

"What does that even mean?" I demanded, frustration bubbling to the surface.

"It means you're both in deep, and the stakes are higher than you think," she replied, her eyes narrowing. "People want what you have, and they're willing to do whatever it takes to get it."

I turned to him, confusion and fear churning inside me. "What have you gotten us into?"

Before he could respond, the bar door swung open with a loud bang, a gust of wind cutting through the haze. A group of men entered, their presence dominating the room. Their faces were hard, etched with the kind of resolve that sent chills racing down my spine. They swept their gazes across the bar, eyes landing on us with predatory intent.

"Shit," he muttered, his expression shifting from determination to alarm. "We need to go. Now."

"Why? Who are they?"

"Let's just say they're not here for happy hour," he snapped, grabbing my hand again, urgency coursing through him. "Follow my lead, and don't look back."

As we weaved through the crowd, the men began advancing, their intentions clear. Panic surged through me, my instincts screaming to run, to hide. But he held tight to my hand, pulling me toward the rear exit as the tension in the air thickened.

We burst out into the alley, the cool night air hitting my face like a splash of cold water. But freedom was short-lived. Just as we turned to sprint away, a harsh voice called from behind us, dripping with menace. "You think you can escape that easily?"

My heart plummeted as I recognized the danger looming over us. The men were right on our heels, closing in fast. Desperation gripped me as we raced down the alley, our breaths mingling with the adrenaline-fueled fear surging through my veins.

"Where now?" I gasped, glancing back to see them gaining ground.

"Trust me!" he shouted, urgency coloring his voice as he pulled me toward a narrow side street, dimly lit and shadowy. "We can lose them in here!"

We darted into the darkness, my pulse pounding as the sounds of our pursuers echoed off the walls. My mind raced with possibilities, dread clenching my stomach. Just as we rounded a corner, the unmistakable sound of footsteps echoed behind us, relentless and predatory.

"Keep running!" he urged, but I felt the weight of fear drag at my feet, each step feeling heavier than the last.

Suddenly, a figure appeared ahead, a silhouette blocking our path. My breath caught in my throat as I recognized the dark outline of a man I had never wanted to see again, a ghost from the past stepping back into my life at the worst possible moment.

"Looks like you're not the only one who's been searching for you," he said, a smirk curling his lips as the shadows engulfed us both.

In that moment, time seemed to freeze, the world narrowing down to that single face, that single choice, as the darkness closed in.

Chapter 13: Collide and Conquer

The air was thick with tension, a palpable charge that made the hair on my arms stand on end. Shadows draped themselves over the sprawling reality show set, which had once buzzed with the vibrant energy of hopeful contestants. Now, it resembled a dark carnival—colorful lights flickering ominously, laughter twisted into echoes of unease, and the ever-present cameras capturing our every move like vultures waiting for a meal. I glanced at him, my reluctant ally, standing close enough that I could smell the faint trace of his cologne, mingling with the acrid scent of fear.

"Do you think they'll really try something?" I whispered, my voice barely breaking the silence, my heart racing as the weight of the moment settled over us.

"They always do," he replied, his tone matter-of-fact, but there was a flicker in his eyes that told me he was just as unsettled. His confidence wavered, a crack in the armor that made him so infuriatingly charming. "But tonight, we've got the upper hand. We know what they want. We know how they think."

"Or at least, we think we know," I countered, my fingers absently tracing the edge of a nearby prop—a faux tropical palm tree that had seen better days. It felt ridiculous to cling to something so mundane in the face of our impending confrontation. "But how do we outsmart someone who's always three steps ahead?"

"By making sure they don't see our next move coming," he said, a grin tugging at the corners of his mouth. "And by being unpredictable."

My heart sank slightly at the thought. He thrived on chaos; I preferred order. But in this game, we were both playing roles that felt foreign and uncomfortable. I studied his face, the light from the neon signs casting playful shadows across his features. There was a determination in his gaze, a flicker of something that resembled hope. I had never thought I'd be here, hiding in the underbelly of this farcical spectacle, sharing a secret plan with a man I had once considered my enemy.

"We could always just walk away," I suggested, though I knew even as I said it that there was no escape. The looming presence of the cameras, the stakes of the competition, and the personal vendetta that had grown between us like a monstrous weed all conspired to keep me tethered to this nightmare.

"Walk away?" He let out a low, incredulous laugh, and it sent a shiver down my spine. "You know better than that. If we walk away, we lose everything. Not just the show, but the chance to take them down."

The thought lingered in the air, heavy and enticing. For all my doubts, the idea of victory—a chance to turn the tables on those who had manipulated and toyed with us—was intoxicating.

"Then what's the plan, oh master strategist?" I teased, hoping to lighten the mood even as my heart pounded in my chest.

"Simple," he replied, stepping closer, the heat of his body radiating towards me. "We create a diversion. Make them think we're about to go after the prize. When they're distracted, we'll slip in and take what we need."

"And how do we create a diversion?" I challenged, feeling my own heart racing as he moved closer.

He leaned in, his breath warm against my cheek, and I felt a flutter of something—anticipation, or perhaps fear. "Let's just say I know a few tricks."

His eyes gleamed with mischief, and I couldn't help but smile despite the gravity of our situation.

"I'm not going to wear a ridiculous costume, am I?" I quipped, trying to shake off the tension, but the absurdity of the situation made me giggle.

"Only if you want to," he replied, a smirk spreading across his face. "But I was thinking more along the lines of some good old-fashioned sabotage."

"Perfect. I can do sabotage," I said, feeling a surge of adrenaline.

Just then, a loud crash echoed through the set, causing us both to jump. My heart raced as I exchanged a glance with him, the moment of levity abruptly severed. "What was that?"

"Looks like our friendly neighborhood villain has decided to make his entrance," he said, his voice low and tense.

We ducked behind a stack of props, hearts pounding in synchrony as we waited. I could hear the sound of footsteps approaching, accompanied by low murmurs that hinted at the chaos unfolding just outside our hiding place. I strained my ears, trying to catch snippets of conversation, but the words were muffled, a language of dread that sent my imagination spiraling.

"Are you ready?" he asked, his eyes locking onto mine, and I could see the intensity there—a mixture of determination and a hint of something softer, something that made my heart swell in a way I hadn't expected.

"Ready as I'll ever be," I whispered, my breath hitching slightly as I caught his gaze. In that moment, with danger looming just outside our makeshift fortress, I felt the undeniable bond between us tighten. It was as if the world had shrunk to just the two of us, suspended in time, waiting for the right moment to strike.

"Let's do this," he said, the bravado in his voice igniting a fire within me. And with that, we sprang into action, a united front against whatever awaited us in the shadows. As we emerged from the concealment of the props, I felt an exhilaration that tinged the edges of fear—a spark of defiance that promised both peril and the possibility of victory.

We stepped into the chaos, hearts racing, minds buzzing with the thrill of the unknown. The dimly lit set was now a disorienting maze, and every turn held the promise of danger. I could hear muffled voices carrying through the air, laced with urgency and whispers of betrayal, as shadows flitted by—figures both familiar and alien weaving through the darkness. A chill swept through me, but it was tempered by the warmth of his presence at my side.

"Just follow my lead," he murmured, his voice barely above a whisper, the seriousness of his tone contrasting sharply with the playful banter we had shared moments before. His confidence grounded me, even as uncertainty gnawed at my insides. I nodded, taking a deep breath, and we moved forward, blending into the tumult.

As we navigated the set, the atmosphere crackled with a sense of anticipation. The cameras, ever watchful, recorded our every move, capturing our fear and determination like a modern-day gladiatorial arena. I couldn't shake the feeling that we were performers in someone else's twisted play, and all it would take was one wrong step for the curtain to fall.

He led me to a cluster of barrels used for some forgotten staging, and we ducked behind them just as two figures passed by. Their laughter rang hollow, echoing off the metal and plastic of the props, a sound that twisted in my gut. I caught a glimpse of one of them—a glint of a familiar face. It was Tara, the queen bee of our cohort, her long hair swinging like a banner as she strutted, a confident smile plastered across her face. She exuded an air of authority, oblivious to the chaos her reign had caused.

"Did you hear about the twist?" she said, her voice dripping with that saccharine sweetness that made my skin crawl. "They're changing the rules again. What's a show without a little more drama, right?"

"Unbelievable," I whispered, my stomach churning. "We're all just pawns in their game."

His jaw clenched, but there was a glimmer of mischief in his eyes. "Let them play their game. We'll play ours."

I watched him as he strategized, his mind racing through possibilities. Despite the fear that lurked in the corners of my mind, I felt a thrill course through me at the sight of his determination. There was a spark between us that ignited my senses, and for a moment, the impending confrontation faded away. It was just us against the world.

"Okay, what's the plan?" I whispered, leaning closer, the closeness amplifying the electric tension swirling in the air.

"Distract them," he said, a slow grin spreading across his face, the kind that made my heart skip. "You're going to make a scene."

"Me? Make a scene?" I laughed incredulously. "That's not really my style."

"Exactly. That's why it'll work," he insisted, his eyes glinting with playful challenge. "They won't expect it. You'll be the wild card."

"I'm flattered," I replied dryly, but the pulse of adrenaline was unmistakable. "What if I flop?"

"Flopping would be the least of our worries," he said, the grin broadening, making me feel as if I were standing on the edge of a cliff, ready to leap. "Trust me, if you flop, I'll be right there to catch you."

I couldn't help but smile back, despite the absurdity of it all. "You know, if we survive this, I might just have to reconsider our entire partnership."

"Just remember to make it a good show," he replied, winking as he stepped back, giving me room to shine—or to utterly fail.

With a deep breath, I stepped away from the safety of our hiding spot and headed towards the heart of the set, where the chaos reigned. The lights were bright and dizzying, the cameras capturing every moment like predators ready to pounce. I focused on Tara and her entourage, my heart thumping loudly in my chest as I approached.

"Hey, Tara!" I called out, my voice cutting through the noise. The crowd turned, surprise flickering across their faces. "Why don't you tell everyone about your plans for the final challenge?"

She blinked, clearly caught off guard. "What do you mean?"

"The plans!" I pressed, putting on a dramatic flair, my inner diva coming to life. "The last-minute twist. Surely, you have something up your sleeve. The world is dying to know!"

The onlookers exchanged confused glances, and I could see Tara scrambling to regain her composure, her smile tightening. "Oh, please, it's just for show," she replied, but there was an edge to her voice that betrayed her uncertainty.

"Just for show?" I exclaimed, raising my voice for added effect. "I don't think so! With all the chaos happening, I bet you have something sinister planned!"

Laughter erupted from the crowd, and the atmosphere shifted. I reveled in the attention, the thrill of being the unexpected center of focus electrifying. The laughter intensified, and I played off it, turning up the heat.

"Let's be real here. You're the queen of chaos, Tara. What's the fun without a little danger? Aren't you going to take us on one last wild ride?"

The words flowed from me like a river, each sentence pulling the crowd deeper into the performance. The tension twisted and coiled, both exhilarating and terrifying.

I didn't notice him approaching until he was beside me, his presence a warm anchor. "You're good at this," he murmured, admiration clear in his voice. "Just keep them distracted a little longer."

I flashed him a quick grin, but my mind raced with the possibilities. This wasn't just a distraction anymore; it was a chance to turn the tide, to reclaim our narrative from those who sought to control it.

The atmosphere was electric, the crowd's energy feeding my resolve. I leaned into the chaos, weaving tales of conspiracy and danger, every word punctuated by the gleam of excitement in their eyes. "And let's not forget about the underdog team—the ones you keep overlooking! We have some tricks up our sleeves too!"

Tara's face darkened, her control slipping as she shot me a glare that could burn a hole through steel. But her reaction only fueled the fire of the audience, who began to murmur among themselves, eager to see how the drama would unfold.

"Maybe it's time for a little reckoning, huh?" I called out, challenging her directly, and the crowd roared in response, the air thick with a sense of rebellion.

And in that moment, I realized: this wasn't just about survival. It was about reclaiming our power, about standing up to those who sought to manipulate us. I glanced sideways at him, who was watching me with a mix of awe and encouragement, and suddenly, the stakes felt higher than ever. The true battle was just beginning, and I was more than ready to fight.

The crowd erupted in a cacophony of cheers and gasps, their energy pulsating like a living entity, feeding off the absurd spectacle I had inadvertently created. I played my role with wild abandon, reveling in the thrill of attention while casting furtive glances at Tara, whose face had morphed into a mask of annoyance and disbelief. I had ignited a fire within the audience, and there was no way I was going to extinguish it now.

"Come on, Tara! Surely you can do better than that," I taunted, my heart racing as I stepped closer, allowing the moment to simmer. "You've been running this show like a well-oiled machine, but it seems you've forgotten one crucial detail: we're still here, and we're not backing down."

"Enough!" she finally snapped, but the cracks in her composure were beginning to show. The audience was buzzing with excitement, the thrill of rebellion coursing through the air like electricity.

"Enough?" I echoed, arching an eyebrow. "Don't you think we deserve a little drama? After all, that's what the fans love, right?"

The cameras zoomed in, capturing every twist of my lips and every spark of defiance in my eyes. I had become an unexpected heroine in this ludicrous play, and the exhilaration fueled me.

As Tara struggled to maintain control, I caught sight of him at the edge of the crowd, watching with an intensity that sent shivers down my spine. He had a smirk playing on his lips, clearly enjoying the spectacle, and his gaze held mine for a heartbeat longer than necessary. The moment grounded me, a reminder that I wasn't in this alone.

But then, just as the tides seemed to shift in our favor, the atmosphere changed, thickening with tension. An ominous presence slithered through the set, and I turned to find the source. A group of production staff, their expressions grim, had formed a barrier at the back, blocking any exit. Panic bubbled just below the surface, and I felt my pulse quicken.

"What's happening?" I muttered, my voice barely audible over the chaos.

"Looks like they're getting ready to shut this down," he said, his tone a mix of disbelief and frustration.

"What do you mean? This is our moment!"

"Maybe, but they don't see it that way."

Before I could respond, the head producer stepped forward, his presence commanding and intimidating. "That's enough!" he barked, cutting through the noise with a voice like thunder. The audience quieted, the energy shifting from euphoric to tense. "We need to end this charade before it spirals out of control."

"Charade?" I scoffed, emboldened by adrenaline. "You think what's happening here is a joke? People are finally standing up for themselves. We're not just props in your little reality show anymore!"

He narrowed his eyes, a mix of irritation and surprise crossing his features. "You want to be heard? Fine. But if you continue this, there will be consequences."

The crowd murmured, and I could feel the weight of their anticipation hanging in the air like fog, thick and suffocating. I caught a glimpse of Tara, her confidence faltering as she realized her grip was slipping. My heart raced at the thought of what was about to happen next.

"Consequences?" I shot back, my voice rising again. "Is that all you've got? We're not afraid of consequences; we're afraid of being silenced! This is our chance to take control, to show the world that we're not just here for your entertainment!"

The crowd erupted into applause, my words reverberating through the throng. I felt emboldened, but the producer remained unfazed, as if he had anticipated this uprising.

"Enough!" he shouted, raising his hand. "If you think you can create a scene here and get away with it, you're sorely mistaken. This show will go on, and if you don't fall in line, you'll be out."

I froze, the air suddenly thick with the gravity of his threat. My mind raced. Did he mean we'd be eliminated from the competition? Or was there something more sinister at play?

"Wait a minute!" a voice called from the back—Sarah, my friend from the earlier days of the show. "This isn't right! We deserve to have a say! If they want to treat us like puppets, then we should cut the strings!"

A wave of agreement surged through the crowd, and I felt a thrill of solidarity. Maybe this was the moment we could seize our narrative, rewriting our roles in this story.

"Right!" I shouted, channeling the energy of the moment. "If they think we're just going to roll over and accept their rules, they're in for a rude awakening! We're not just contestants; we're a force!"

The cheers were deafening, drowning out the producer's protests. But just as it seemed we might overpower the situation, the power suddenly cut out—the lights flickering ominously before plunging us into darkness.

Gasps echoed, and I felt a surge of panic. "What's happening?" I shouted, but my voice was swallowed by the chaos.

Then, in the heart of the darkness, I heard a sinister laugh—a sound so chilling it sent a shiver down my spine. "Did you really think you could get away with this?"

My heart pounded as I squinted into the blackness, struggling to see the source of the voice. "Who's there?" I called, my voice trembling despite my attempts to sound brave.

"Your little rebellion has consequences," the voice taunted, cold and cruel, slithering through the darkness like a serpent. "And you're about to find out just how far you've gone."

I felt him step closer, the warmth of his body beside me as he whispered urgently, "We need to get out of here. Now."

The lights flickered back on, but chaos erupted around us. People were scrambling, and I could see panic etched across their faces. In that moment, it became clear that whatever game had been set into motion was far more dangerous than we had anticipated.

"Stay close," he urged, and as we maneuvered through the throng, I felt the weight of the danger settling in.

But just as we reached the exit, a hand shot out from the shadows, gripping my arm. "You're not going anywhere!" The voice was deep and menacing, and I felt a jolt of fear.

"Let go of her!" he shouted, but the grip tightened, pulling me back into the depths of chaos.

And in that instant, everything spiraled out of control. The world around me blurred into a whirlwind of sound and movement, and I realized with dawning horror that we had only begun to scratch the surface of the darkness that lay ahead.

Chapter 14: A Breath from the Grave

A silence cloaked the room, thick and suffocating, as I stared at my phone, the screen glowing ominously in the darkness. My heart raced, hammering against my ribcage like a prisoner desperate for freedom. I knew that voice all too well, a sinister echo from a past I had fought tooth and nail to escape. It was a chilling reminder that some shadows never fade, that some enemies lurk just beyond the edges of our bravest moments, waiting for the perfect opportunity to pounce.

"Why now?" I whispered into the silence, not expecting an answer. The walls of my small apartment felt as if they were closing in, the air heavy with the scent of stale coffee and anxiety. I ran a hand through my hair, the familiar tang of panic spiking my adrenaline. I should have been asleep, lost in the sweet oblivion of dreams, but there was no room for fantasy when reality bore down like a relentless storm.

"Not done with you yet." The words dripped with malice, each syllable a thread weaving my nightmares into a living tapestry of dread. I sank into my worn-out armchair, the upholstery threadbare but still comforting, a sanctuary I had claimed for myself after the chaos of the last few months. Outside, the wind howled like a ghost seeking revenge, and the trees danced with a frantic energy, branches clawing at the night sky as if trying to escape the very earth that held them down.

I inhaled sharply, the cool air slicing through the haze of my thoughts. My phone slipped from my fingers, landing with a soft thud on the carpet, its vibration a reminder that the world outside kept spinning, oblivious to my turmoil. Each breath felt like a fight, a battle against the creeping darkness that threatened to consume me whole. I had made choices, sacrifices even, to sever the ties that bound me to that part of my life. And now, here he was, clawing his way back in, like a snake shedding its skin, more venomous than ever.

It wasn't just my life at stake; it was the fragile peace I had fought to maintain. My friends, my family, they all depended on me. I had dragged them through hell already, and I wasn't about to lead them back into the inferno. But what could I do against a specter of such wrath? He knew my weaknesses, my fears. He knew how to pull the strings of my existence, orchestrating a symphony of chaos designed to break me.

I bolted upright, a sense of determination surging through me like wildfire. No more hiding, no more waiting for the storm to pass. I had to confront this darkness head-on, armed with the knowledge that I had allies, friends who wouldn't let me face this alone. Their unwavering support had been my beacon through the murkiest of waters. I could already envision Olivia's fierce gaze, her fiery spirit a warm embrace against the cold chill of despair. She would stand beside me, her unwavering strength grounding me, a reminder that I wasn't alone in this fight.

I grabbed my phone, heart racing, and dialed her number. The ringing felt like a countdown, each tone echoing in the silence of my apartment. When she finally answered, her voice was a soothing balm against the razor edge of my anxiety. "What's wrong?"

"It's him," I replied, my voice barely above a whisper. "He's back. He called."

The pause on the other end was heavy, like a weighted blanket pressing down on my chest. "Are you sure? It could be a prank, a sick joke."

I shook my head, even though she couldn't see me. "No joke. I recognized his voice. He's out for blood, Liv. And I don't think he'll stop until he gets what he wants."

"What does he want?" she asked, her voice now laced with urgency.

"Me. Us. Everything we've built together. He wants to tear it all down."

"Then we'll stop him. Together." Her resolve was like a lifeline, a promise forged in the fires of our shared experiences. I could almost hear her pacing in her own apartment, calculating, plotting.

"Do you remember the old warehouse on Main Street?" I asked, an idea sparking to life. It was a relic of the past, a crumbling structure that had once served as a hideout for the nefarious dealings of our adversaries. Now it was a ghost of its former self, a perfect place to lay low and plan our next move.

"I do," she replied, her voice steady. "It'll be a risk, but if he's watching us, we'll need to lure him out, draw him into the open where we can get the upper hand."

"Exactly. I'll meet you there at dawn. We can set up a strategy, figure out how to turn the tables."

I hung up the phone, my heart still racing, but now with a sense of purpose igniting a fire within me. The shadows no longer felt quite so suffocating. This was my moment to reclaim my narrative, to take back what he had stolen from me—my peace, my safety, my life.

As the night deepened around me, I gathered my things, feeling the weight of my resolve settle into place. I couldn't allow the echoes of my past to dictate my future. It was time to rise from the ashes, to confront the specter of my fears with the same fierceness that had carried me through so many trials. With a newfound determination, I stepped into the night, ready to embrace the battle that lay ahead.

The first light of dawn spilled through my window like molten gold, painting the walls with hues of optimism that felt almost mocking. I sat on the edge of my bed, heart still thrumming with the remnants of last night's terror. The stillness of the morning was deceptive, the calm before a storm I had unwittingly invited. I had barely slept, haunted by fragmented memories of the voice that threatened to unravel everything I had rebuilt. The phone call replayed in my mind, each word laced with venom, a reminder that monsters don't always hide under the bed; sometimes, they call you directly.

I glanced around my apartment, now a jumble of half-packed bags and hastily scribbled notes. The clutter felt oppressive, a physical manifestation of the chaos in my mind. I had plans, I had hope, but I also had a very real enemy lurking in the shadows, ready to strike when I least expected it. I needed clarity, a strategy, and most importantly, the unwavering support of my friends. The warehouse was a relic of our past, but it would serve as our battlefield—a place where we could confront our demons together.

The sun crested higher, and with it came a jolt of energy. I slipped into my favorite leather jacket, its well-worn fabric a comfort against the chill of the morning air. Each movement felt deliberate, each step toward the door a declaration of my intent. I was no longer a victim, cowering under the weight of fear. I was a fighter, and it was time to reclaim my narrative.

As I drove to the warehouse, the streets were still slick with morning dew, the world waking up slowly around me. I turned up the radio, allowing the upbeat music to drown out the nagging doubts creeping into my mind. The car hummed with life, a stark contrast to the dead silence that had enveloped me just hours before. It felt good to sing along, to lose myself in a rhythm that urged me forward instead of backward.

Arriving at the warehouse, I parked and stepped out into the embrace of a brisk breeze. The building loomed ahead, a monolith of crumbling brick and rusted metal, remnants of a time long past. The air was heavy with the scent of old wood and rain-soaked earth, a grounding reminder that even in decay, there could be strength. I approached the entrance, the door creaking ominously as I pushed it open, revealing a cavernous interior filled with shadows and echoes.

Inside, Olivia was already there, her silhouette outlined by the dull morning light filtering through shattered windows. She turned, a fierce look in her eyes that melted into a smile as she spotted me. "You made it," she said, a playful lilt in her voice that was both a relief and a challenge. "I was worried you'd get scared off."

"Me? Scared?" I laughed, though the sound felt hollow. "I'd sooner take on a pack of rabid raccoons than let that creep intimidate me."

"Good to know," she smirked, leaning against a rusted beam. "I brought coffee. Not the best kind, but it's definitely strong enough to wake the dead."

"Perfect," I said, following her to a makeshift table. A thermos sat beside a scattering of notes and maps—our battle plan in the making. The aroma of the coffee filled the air, grounding me, giving me a sense of purpose. We poured two steaming cups, the warmth spreading through my fingers like a comforting embrace.

"Okay," she began, her voice shifting to a serious tone. "What's the game plan? We know he's watching. He'll be expecting us to panic, to retreat. We can't let him have that satisfaction."

"Right. We need to draw him out, make him think he has the upper hand." I took a sip of the coffee, the bitterness jolting me awake. "What if we stage a distraction? Something big enough to lure him in but controlled enough to keep us safe."

"Like a fake deal? Something that would be irresistible to him?" Olivia's eyes sparkled with mischief, her strategist mind whirring. "We could set up a meeting, maybe even use some of his old contacts. They'd be perfect bait."

"That could work." I leaned closer, a plan forming in my mind. "If we play our cards right, we can turn this into a trap. We use his greed against him. He'll think he's winning, but we'll have the upper hand."

The excitement in the air was palpable, our shared energy igniting a spark of hope amidst the looming darkness. As we jotted down ideas and potential contacts, the atmosphere transformed from one of despair to one of determination. It was in these moments that I remembered the strength we wielded together, the bonds forged in the fires of past battles.

But beneath that sense of camaraderie, a shadow flickered at the edges of my consciousness—a reminder that plans often have a way of unraveling. The stakes were higher this time, and I could feel the weight of every decision pressing down on my shoulders. Would we be ready when the moment came? Would we be enough?

Suddenly, the sound of footsteps echoed outside, breaking our focused chatter. A shiver ran down my spine as we exchanged glances, tension coiling in the air. Olivia grabbed my arm, her grip firm. "Do you think it's him?"

"I don't know," I whispered, my heart pounding in sync with the footsteps growing closer. "We need to be ready for anything."

The door creaked open, and I braced myself for confrontation, my heart racing as the figure stepped inside. But it wasn't the face I had anticipated. Instead, a familiar silhouette emerged from the shadows, an unexpected ally I hadn't seen in months. "You two look like you've been planning a heist," Ryan said, a lopsided grin spreading across his face.

"Ryan!" I exclaimed, a rush of relief flooding through me. "What are you doing here?"

"I heard you might need backup," he said, stepping further into the light. His presence was a welcome surprise, a reminder that we were not alone in this fight.

Olivia smirked, her gaze shifting between us. "Well, you're just in time for some coffee and chaos. Care to join?"

Ryan chuckled, his eyes sparkling with mischief. "I wouldn't miss it for the world. Let's turn this heist into a full-on operation."

As we gathered around the table, a new energy surged through the room. It was an unexpected twist in a plot that had already spiraled out of control, but that was the essence of our battle—embracing the chaos and using it to our advantage. Together, we would not only confront the darkness but turn it into our ally.

The atmosphere in the warehouse shifted as Ryan joined us, his presence invigorating yet filled with an undercurrent of tension. We quickly filled him in on the situation, our voices a hurried symphony of plans and worries. Ryan listened intently, his brow furrowed in concentration as he absorbed the details. "So, we're really doing this, then? Going back to the scene of the crime?" He leaned against the table, crossing his arms, his posture relaxed but his eyes sharp.

"Exactly," I said, a spark of defiance igniting within me. "We're not going to let him dictate our lives anymore. If he thinks he can control the narrative, he's got another thing coming."

"I like it," Ryan replied, nodding appreciatively. "Taking the fight to him. It's almost poetic in a tragic sort of way."

"Poetic? I prefer to think of it as a grand finale," Olivia chimed in, her enthusiasm infectious. "We'll lure him out, give him a show he won't forget. With any luck, we'll have him right where we want him."

"Just remember, no actual fireworks," I said, trying to inject some levity into the tension. "I'd rather not blow us all up in the process."

"Agreed," Ryan said with a mock-serious expression. "Let's save the explosions for when we've got him cornered. Preferably with some clever traps or an elaborate scheme that would make a villain jealous."

We spent the next few hours drafting plans and sketches, turning the warehouse into a battleground in our minds. The morning light streamed through the broken windows, illuminating the dust motes that danced in the air, a tangible reminder of our shared history in this forgotten space. It was a canvas for our intentions, a place where we could carve out a strategy and confront the specters of our past.

"Okay, let's talk specifics," I said, setting down my coffee mug. "If we want to make this convincing, we'll need a distraction. Something big enough to draw him out but not so reckless that it puts us at risk."

Olivia tilted her head, a thoughtful frown creasing her brow. "What if we create a scenario that looks like a deal gone bad? Something he'd be drawn to. We could set up a fake meeting with one of his old associates, someone he trusts."

Ryan leaned in, his fingers tapping against the table rhythmically. "I know someone who might be able to help. A contact who could impersonate that associate. He owes me a favor and loves a bit of chaos."

I raised an eyebrow, intrigued. "Chaos is right up our alley. What's the plan?"

Ryan grinned, his enthusiasm contagious. "I can get him to agree to a meet at the old docks. It's secluded, but still busy enough to look legitimate. We make it seem like a high-stakes transaction. Once he shows up, we can spring the trap."

"Perfect." I felt a rush of adrenaline at the thought of finally flipping the script on our adversary. "We'll need to set up cameras, too. Document everything, just in case."

With a shared sense of purpose, we laid out our roles and responsibilities, the atmosphere electric with anticipation. The clock ticked away as we strategized, bouncing ideas off one another until our plan began to take shape, intricate and daring. But as the sun climbed higher, a gnawing sense of dread coiled in my stomach. We were edging toward a confrontation, and the stakes had never felt higher.

"What if he sees through our ruse?" I asked, my voice barely above a whisper. "What if he's already anticipating our moves?"

Ryan's gaze sharpened, the laughter fading from his eyes. "Then we adapt. We have to stay one step ahead. Trust in the element of surprise. We'll be ready for anything."

"Exactly," Olivia added, her voice steadying me. "We've come too far to turn back now. This is about more than just us—it's about taking back control."

With the plan solidified, we packed our gear, each item a reminder of the battle ahead. I couldn't shake the feeling of impending doom that lurked just beyond the edges of my thoughts. The past was a relentless specter, whispering doubts into my ear, but I shoved those feelings aside, willing myself to focus on the here and now.

As dusk approached, the three of us made our way to the docks, the air thick with anticipation. The sun dipped below the horizon, casting long shadows that danced eerily against the water's surface. The docks were eerily quiet, the sounds of the city muted in the growing darkness. Each step felt heavy, the weight of our mission pressing down on us.

"I can't shake this feeling," I murmured, glancing around. "What if this all goes sideways?"

Ryan chuckled softly, his voice low. "That's the thrill of it, isn't it? The risk. Besides, you've already faced worse. Remember that time you almost set fire to your kitchen?"

"Touché," I replied, a small smile breaking through the tension. "Let's hope tonight doesn't involve any flames."

As we set up the equipment—cameras, microphones, the whole gambit—an uneasy tension filled the air. Each sound felt amplified; the creak of the old wooden beams, the gentle lap of water against the docks, and the whisper of the wind carried an undercurrent of danger.

Just as we completed our setup, a low rumble echoed through the night, causing my heart to quicken. "What was that?" I asked, scanning the area.

"Just the train, probably," Olivia suggested, but her voice lacked conviction.

"No. This is different." Ryan's eyes narrowed, his instincts kicking in. "It's too close."

A shiver of apprehension ran down my spine as we huddled together, the distant sound of tires crunching on gravel approaching rapidly. My heart raced, and I motioned for silence. The headlights of a vehicle cut through the darkness, illuminating our hiding spot.

"We're not ready," I whispered, panic bubbling in my throat.

"We can't back down now," Ryan urged, his grip firm on my shoulder. "We'll stand our ground."

As the vehicle came to a halt, the sound of doors slamming echoed in the night, a promise of confrontation lurking just beyond the reach of our concealed position. I could see shadows moving, silhouettes that felt familiar yet menacing. The atmosphere shifted, a heavy silence settling around us, thick with unspoken words and the weight of what was to come.

Then a voice rang out, cutting through the darkness like a knife. "I know you're here! You think you can play games with me?"

A chill ran down my spine, and I turned to Olivia, my breath hitching in my throat. "It's him. He's found us."

As the shadows drew closer, the realization dawned—our carefully laid plans were crumbling before us. I took a step back, fear tightening its grip around my chest, but there was no turning back now. The air crackled with anticipation as we braced ourselves for the inevitable confrontation, the night closing in around us like a shroud.

"Get ready," I whispered, adrenaline coursing through my veins. "This is it."

But before we could react, a loud crash erupted from behind us, the sound of shattering glass ringing out like a death knell. I spun around, heart in my throat, only to find a familiar face emerging from the shadows—someone I never expected to see again, someone whose presence could either save us or spell our doom.

"Surprise!" they exclaimed, a twisted grin spreading across their face.

My heart sank as the world around me tilted precariously, a precarious cliffhanger that left me teetering on the edge of uncertainty.

Chapter 15: Broken Promises

The air around me crackled with the remnants of our unspoken words, and I couldn't shake the feeling that the world had shifted on its axis. I stood rooted to the spot, my heart pounding in my chest like a desperate drum, each beat echoing the void he left behind. The sun crept up lazily over the skyline, spilling gold across the concrete jungle, illuminating the fragments of our past like confetti in the harsh light of reality. Each memory felt like a tiny cut; beautiful but painful, reminding me of what had been.

I turned slowly, scanning the city that had once felt like our playground. The coffee shop on the corner where we'd spent countless hours laughing over frothy lattes now seemed like a hollow monument to our dreams. It was the place where we'd first met, where I had miscalculated the froth-to-espresso ratio and splattered my first order all over his pristine shirt. He had laughed, a warm, infectious sound that made me forget my embarrassment. "Nice to meet you, Coffee Disaster," he'd teased, and in that moment, I was captivated.

Now, that laughter was just a ghost, lingering like perfume on a forgotten scarf. I took a deep breath, letting the scent of fresh bread from the bakery waft over me, grounding me in the present. Maybe I should move on, let the wind carry my pain away like fallen leaves. But how do you let go of someone who knows your soul?

As I wandered aimlessly down the bustling street, the voices of morning commuters washed over me—each laugh, each exclamation felt like a weight pressing down on my heart. I ducked into the small florist tucked between two towering glass buildings, the vibrant colors and fragrant blooms a stark contrast to my gloomy thoughts. The bell jingled softly as I entered, and I was met with the comforting sight of hydrangeas bursting forth in hues of blue and lavender, their petals vibrant and lush.

"Hey there!" the florist called, her smile as bright as the sun streaming through the window. "You look like you could use some cheer. Can I interest you in something? A bouquet perhaps?"

I offered her a weak smile, the corners of my mouth barely lifting. "Just browsing, thanks."

"Sometimes, just browsing isn't enough," she said, her tone playful, but her eyes held a knowing kindness. "A little color can do wonders for the soul."

"Tell me about it," I muttered under my breath, but the words slipped out louder than I intended. She cocked an eyebrow, and I knew I'd have to explain myself, if only to satisfy her curiosity.

"My boyfriend just left me," I confessed, the admission rolling off my tongue like a bitter pill. "Or should I say ex-boyfriend?"

"Ah, the classic tale of love gone awry," she replied, her hands still busy arranging flowers. "You know, I've had my fair share of heartbreaks. It's tough, but it can also lead to something beautiful."

"Like what?" I shot back, the words tumbling out before I could catch them. "A more vibrant collection of florals?"

"Perhaps. Or perhaps it leads you to a newfound strength you didn't know you had," she said, glancing up at me with an understanding that made me feel seen. "And sometimes, it leads to a better version of yourself."

I rolled my eyes, feeling a mix of exasperation and gratitude. "Or it leads to a cat named Whiskers and a lifetime supply of ice cream. But hey, whatever works."

Her laughter rang out, a melodic sound that broke through my fog. "I think you'll find it's all about perspective. Do you have a cat?"

"No," I admitted, "but I do have a penchant for procrastinating. And here I am, trying to delay the inevitable breakdown that's waiting for me at home."

"Home is overrated," she replied with a mischievous grin. "Why don't you take a few blooms? I'll give you a discount. It's hard to stay sad when you're surrounded by flowers."

I considered it, her words hanging in the air like a delicate thread. "Alright, throw in some of those bright yellow daisies. They look cheerful enough to distract me."

As she prepared the bouquet, I felt a little spark of joy flicker in my chest. Maybe it was the flowers or the florist's infectious spirit, but something inside me began to thaw. I paid her, grateful for the tiny reprieve she had offered me, and stepped back out onto the street, the weight of my heart still heavy, but not entirely unbearable.

I walked with purpose, my mind swirling like the petals in my hand, contemplating the future that stretched ahead, uncertain yet enticing. The city felt alive around me, filled with possibilities. If I could just allow the vibrant colors of the daisies to seep into my heart, perhaps I could find a new path, a new purpose.

But as I rounded the corner, I was jolted by a familiar figure emerging from a coffee shop, his expression a mixture of surprise and hesitation. Time seemed to freeze, the vibrant world around us fading into a dull hue as I locked eyes with him. The air thickened with unspoken words, and the daisies trembled slightly in my grasp, as if echoing the uncertainty swirling between us. Would I break my silence, or would we stand there, two souls adrift in a sea of past promises?

The air shifted again, filled with a mix of apprehension and longing as I stood frozen, clutching the daisies like a lifeline. He didn't move, a fleeting moment stretching into infinity as our gazes clashed in a tumult of emotions—confusion, regret, and a desperate flicker of hope. I could feel my heart racing, a thundering echo against the quiet chaos of the street.

"Fancy meeting you here," he finally said, his voice laced with a bemusement that could only come from an awkward reunion. The way he said it, half-joking and half-serious, made me wonder if he felt the weight of the past as much as I did.

"Right," I replied, trying to sound nonchalant as I shifted my grip on the bouquet. "Just taking a stroll with my floral therapy session. You know how it is—daisies and denial, my two best friends."

His lips quirked up at the corners, but his eyes remained serious. "I didn't think you were the flower type."

"And I didn't think you were the 'walk away without saying goodbye' type." My words came out sharper than I intended, the hurt edging into my tone like an unwelcome guest crashing the party.

He rubbed the back of his neck, a familiar gesture that once used to soothe me, now serving only to heighten the tension between us. "Look, I didn't plan for this to happen."

"Neither did I." I took a step closer, emboldened by the daisies' sunny optimism, my courage swelling like a tide. "But here we are, practically scripted in a rom-com, except there's no soundtrack and the punchlines are all delivered wrong."

He let out a short laugh, a sound that felt like a balm on my raw nerves. "Yeah, well, life doesn't always come with a charming lead-in."

"Or a script," I countered, emboldened by the unexpected levity. "And definitely not a happy ending."

The silence stretched between us again, laden with unspoken thoughts. The city buzzed around us, oblivious to our quiet standoff. A couple ambled past, hand in hand, their carefree laughter contrasting sharply with our unresolved tension. I envied them, the ease of their connection and the simplicity of their moment.

"I've been thinking about what happened," he finally said, his gaze steady, searching. "About us."

"Really? Because it didn't seem like it on your way out the door." I couldn't help but fire back, my heart racing as the words spilled from my lips. "Just a text and a shadow, and poof—you were gone."

"Do you think it was easy for me?" His frustration cracked through the surface, revealing a vulnerability I hadn't seen before. "I didn't want it to end like this, but I felt like I was drowning. I didn't know how to breathe around you anymore."

The honesty in his words struck me, resonating like a tuning fork in my chest. "So, what? You thought running away was the answer?"

"Maybe I thought you'd be better off without me. I didn't want to pull you down with me." His expression hardened for a moment, but I could see the flicker of regret dancing behind his eyes.

"Congratulations, you've officially achieved the 'hero complex,'" I quipped, my tone lighter than my heart felt. "What was I supposed to do? Sit around and wait for you to figure it out? That's not my style."

"No, you're the daisy type—always blooming despite the storms," he said, a hint of admiration creeping into his voice.

"Touché," I replied, rolling my eyes at the poetic nonsense that felt oddly comforting. "But daisies don't thrive in neglect, you know. They need care, sunlight, and the occasional sprinkle of optimism."

"Maybe I didn't know how to give you that," he admitted, his voice softening. "I was scared, alright? Scared of what we could become."

"Or what you might lose?" I asked, the tension dissipating slightly as understanding began to weave its way through our words. "You were scared of being vulnerable."

He met my gaze, the intensity of his expression unraveling the tension that had bound us. "Can't say I blame you for wanting to run from me. I didn't exactly play the role of the trustworthy boyfriend."

"Trust is a two-way street," I countered gently, feeling the flicker of hope rekindle within me. "But I wanted to figure it out with you. I didn't want to walk away from everything we had."

The honesty hung in the air, fragile yet potent, like the bouquet in my hand, its petals brushing softly against my palm. "I miss us," I admitted, the confession slipping from my lips before I could stop it. "And maybe I'm just a fool for thinking we could still find a way back."

He took a step closer, the distance between us shrinking until I could almost feel the warmth radiating from him. "You're not a fool," he said, his voice low, steady. "You're brave for wanting to try again. I just... I need to know if you're willing to take the leap with me."

"Leap?" I echoed, my heart racing with uncertainty. "That's a pretty big ask, especially after you just bolted."

"Yeah, I know." He ran a hand through his hair, a familiar gesture that made my stomach twist. "But I'm asking for a second chance. I want to show you that I can be better. That we can be better."

In that moment, my mind raced, weighing the possibilities, the risks, the potential for heartbreak against the warmth of his sincerity. I remembered the laughter, the shared dreams, and the ease of being with him, how the world felt brighter when he was near. "So you're suggesting we jump into the unknown together?"

He nodded, a flicker of hope sparking in his eyes. "Together."

I took a deep breath, letting the weight of my decision settle in. The daisies, bright and defiant, seemed to echo my thoughts, urging me to embrace the possibility of renewal. "Okay," I finally said, my voice barely above a whisper. "Let's take that leap, but no more running, alright?"

A smile broke across his face, genuine and bright, and in that instant, the air around us shifted again. The promise of something new, something fragile yet beautiful, hung between us, ready to unfold like the petals of my daisies—tender, full of potential, waiting for the sun to shine.

The moment lingered, a fragile heartbeat in the expanse of the city around us. As his eyes met mine, the world began to dissolve—no honking horns, no bustling pedestrians, just the two of us suspended in this delicate bubble of time. I could see the conflict churning within him, a tempest behind those dark eyes, and a sudden surge of determination welled up within me.

"Together, then," I reiterated, my heart pounding like a war drum. "But if we're doing this, we're doing it right. No more running, no more hiding behind walls. Just... honesty."

His gaze softened, and the hint of a smile broke through, warming the chilly morning air. "Honesty. Got it. So, does that mean I can ask what you really think of my coffee-making skills?"

I laughed, the tension breaking like a fragile thread. "Let's just say your froth art leaves much to be desired. But your ability to walk away from a conversation? Ten out of ten."

He feigned offense, a playful glimmer sparking in his eyes. "I'll have you know I perfected the art of avoidance."

"Is that what you call it? Because I was under the impression it was more of a cowardly dash."

"Hey, I can be brave when it counts!" He stepped forward, closing the distance between us. "I mean, I'm here now, aren't I?"

"True," I admitted, feeling a warmth rise in my cheeks. "But just showing up isn't the end of the story. We need to build something here."

"Alright," he said, his expression shifting to one of determination. "Let's build. I want to know what you need from me. What can I do to make this work?"

The question hung between us, heavy yet filled with potential. I thought for a moment, realizing the depth of my own vulnerability. "I need you to be present," I said finally. "No more half-hearted gestures. If we're in this together, I want all of you—flaws and all."

"I can do that," he replied, his voice steady and sincere. "But you have to promise me something too."

"What's that?"

"Promise you won't shy away when things get tough. You can't just run back to your daisies at the first sign of trouble."

"Deal." I smiled, exhilarated by this newfound clarity. The fear that had haunted our last moments together started to dissolve like mist in the sunlight. "But you have to remember that daisies thrive in sunlight, not shadows."

"Then let's keep the sun shining."

Just then, the bells of the nearby church chimed, slicing through the air like a blade, reminding me of the fleeting nature of time. I took a step back, the reality of our conversation washing over me. "Okay, so where do we start?"

He glanced around as if the city itself might provide the answer, then his gaze landed back on me, determination etched on his face. "How about coffee? An actual cup, not just your half-finished order thrown at my feet."

"Are you asking me out for coffee after all this?" I quipped, raising an eyebrow, but my heart fluttered at the notion.

"Absolutely. And this time, I promise not to spill any."

As we turned to leave, the air between us crackled with possibilities, a delicate tension that felt almost electric. The sun was fully awake now, bathing the city in golden light, illuminating a path ahead that was both daunting and exciting. With each step, I could feel the weight of my earlier heartache beginning to lift, replaced by a burgeoning hope.

But just as we reached the corner of the street, a commotion erupted nearby. A figure stumbled out of the alleyway, disheveled and wild-eyed, drawing my attention like a magnet. A heavyset man, clad in an oversized jacket that looked as if it had been stitched together from a dozen different fabrics, lunged toward us.

"Help! Please!" the man gasped, desperation etched into every line of his face. "They're coming for me!"

"What's going on?" I instinctively stepped forward, my heart racing as I scanned the street. The man was trembling, glancing back over his shoulder as if the very shadows might come alive.

"I need you to listen!" he urged, his voice rising in urgency. "I didn't mean to steal the money! They think I have something important!"

"Who?" I asked, bewildered. "Who's coming?"

"Please, they're dangerous!" he pleaded, his eyes wide with fear. "I can't go back, you have to help me!"

I glanced at my companion, whose expression mirrored my own confusion and concern. "We should call the police," he suggested, but the man shook his head vehemently.

"No! They can't know I'm here. You don't understand!" His voice dropped to a frantic whisper. "They're watching. They'll do anything to get what they want. You have to hide me!"

I hesitated, torn between instinct and caution. This wasn't the kind of morning I had envisioned. My heart thudded in my chest, torn between wanting to help and recognizing the danger that lurked just beneath the surface.

As the distant sound of footsteps echoed through the alley, a wave of anxiety washed over me. "We can't just—"

"Trust me!" the man insisted, his voice rising. "You don't want to get involved, but you're already in this now. They'll come for you next!"

I glanced back at him, uncertainty pooling in my stomach. The stakes had suddenly shifted from rekindling a relationship to something far more perilous, and the heat of the moment cast a shadow over the brightness we had just begun to build.

"Okay, fine!" I said, adrenaline fueling my resolve. "But where can we hide you?"

He glanced around, his eyes darting to the nearby storefronts before settling back on us. "I know a place. Just trust me."

With a nod, I took a deep breath, my heart racing at the whirlwind of emotions flooding my system. This wasn't how I envisioned our day starting, but perhaps this was a leap into the unknown we had both been craving. I felt a mix of dread and exhilaration as we rushed toward the alley, a new chapter unfolding, ready to entangle us in ways we couldn't yet foresee.

But just as we rounded the corner, the unmistakable sound of heavy boots echoed ominously behind us, sending a chill racing down my spine. I turned, my breath hitching in my throat, as I caught a glimpse of figures emerging from the shadows. There were more than I'd expected, and they were advancing fast, eyes glinting with an intensity that promised danger.

"Run!" I shouted, adrenaline surging as the reality of our situation dawned on me. The morning sun, once a beacon of hope, now cast long shadows that felt alive, threatening to swallow us whole.

Chapter 16: The Final Reckoning

The day dawns cold, the air thick with anticipation and the weight of unfinished business. The city stands as witness to this final confrontation, the skyscrapers stretching like sentinels, their glass facades reflecting a sky bruised with gray. I breathe in deeply, the chill stinging my lungs, grounding me in the reality of what is to come. This moment has been a long time in the making, each tick of the clock echoing like a drumbeat of fate. I can almost hear the past whispering behind me, a chorus of voices reminding me of every mistake, every decision that led me to this very street corner.

The light shifts, and shadows stretch like fingers reaching for something just out of grasp. He stands across from me, the man who hunted me with a ferocity I can barely comprehend, the architect of chaos who shattered lives without a second thought. Yet here we are, two sides of the same coin, and despite the rage simmering beneath my skin, an unexpected calm envelops me. I can feel the city breathing around us, the pulse of its heartbeat thrumming in sync with my own, as if it knows that something monumental is about to unfold.

"Didn't think you'd actually show up," he calls out, his voice smooth and taunting, laced with that sickening confidence that has always unnerved me. There's a swagger in his stance, a casualness that belies the tension crackling in the air. It infuriates me, stirs something primal and raw that claws its way up from my gut.

"You've underestimated me for the last time," I retort, letting my voice carry across the distance, a challenge wrapped in steel. The words feel like a declaration of war, each syllable charged with the promise of retribution. I step forward, the sharp edge of determination cutting through the fog of uncertainty. My heart beats steadily in my chest, a metronome keeping time with the chaos around us.

He laughs, a hollow sound that ricochets off the buildings. "Oh, please. You think this is about you? This is bigger than you or me. This is a game, and I play to win."

The audacity of his words ignites a fire within me. I won't let him twist this narrative any longer. "You may play your games, but I've become something you can't control. You thought you could break me, but you were wrong." Each word drips with conviction, the truth of my journey pouring out with every breath.

For a moment, I see a flicker of something—fear, perhaps?—in his eyes before he masks it with a grin that could charm the devil. "Ah, the little sparrow thinks she's a phoenix now."

"More like a dragon," I say, unable to suppress the smile tugging at my lips. The absurdity of this situation, the gravity of our words, is almost laughable. Here we are, locked in a duel of wits, and yet I feel the absurdity fade away, replaced by a clarity I didn't know I was searching for.

The air shifts as the wind picks up, sending papers swirling like lost thoughts around us. In that chaos, I see the ghosts of all my choices—my family, my friends, the lives he upended in his insatiable pursuit of power. It's a heavy burden, but it strengthens my resolve. "This ends today, one way or another."

"Bold words for someone standing on the brink of oblivion," he counters, his tone mocking, but beneath it, there's a tremor of uncertainty.

"Oblivion? No. I'm standing on the edge of freedom." With each step forward, I can feel the weight of my past shifting, settling into a solid foundation beneath my feet. This isn't just about revenge; it's about reclaiming everything he tried to steal from me—my power, my narrative, my life.

He takes a step back, momentarily thrown off balance. "You think you can intimidate me? I built my empire on the backs of people like you."

"Your empire is built on lies and manipulation. It's crumbling, and you know it." The truth rings clear between us, a sword drawn in the tense air.

A flicker of doubt dances in his eyes, but he quickly masks it, the mask of confidence slipping back into place. "You'll regret this, little bird."

I chuckle, a sound filled with equal parts mirth and defiance. "You've been saying that for years, and yet here I am, stronger than ever." The moment hangs suspended, and I relish it, a tantalizing taste of victory.

As he readies himself, I can see the gears turning in his mind, a moment of uncertainty creeping in. It's a crack in the facade, an opening. The city seems to hold its breath, the hustle and bustle around us fading into a distant hum. My heart races, and for a brief moment, I feel almost sorry for him. He doesn't realize that I am no longer the frightened girl who ran from shadows; I am the storm he never anticipated.

"Let's end this," I say, my voice steady and resolute, the chill of the day invigorating my spirit. I know this moment is mine to seize, the culmination of everything I have fought for.

With a flick of his wrist, he summons his own forces, a band of shadows that had once felt like an insurmountable wall. But today, they seem like mere obstacles in my path. I can feel the energy shifting, the air thick with impending conflict, a sensation that crackles against my skin.

"I've waited for this moment too long to let it slip away," he snarls, and I realize that, for him, this isn't just a game; it's a lifeline.

I step into the fray, ready to reclaim everything he tried to take from me. The ground beneath me feels solid, and as I face the gathering storm, I can't help but smile. This is my moment, and I will not let it pass me by.

The tension in the air is palpable, thick enough to cut with a knife, and I can feel it wrapping around me like a vice. He's trying to gauge my reaction, searching for a crack in my facade, but I stand tall, anchored by the weight of my choices. My heart pounds, each beat a reminder of the journey that brought me to this precipice, and it feels as if the city itself is holding its breath, waiting for the inevitable clash.

"Do you really think you can win?" His voice drips with condescension, the way an older sibling might speak to a younger one attempting to prove their worth. "This isn't a fairy tale, and you're certainly no knight in shining armor."

"Maybe not, but I'm definitely the one with the sword," I shoot back, a grin forming involuntarily. There's a rush of adrenaline surging through me, igniting a spark of humor amidst the grimness of our confrontation. "And I've had quite enough of your fairy tale, thank you very much."

For a heartbeat, his confidence falters, and I relish the fleeting glimpse of uncertainty flickering in his eyes. But just as quickly, he smooths his expression, masking it beneath a veneer of arrogance. "You've always had a flair for the dramatic, but I assure you, it won't save you this time."

Around us, the city bustles in oblivious chaos. Horns blare, voices chatter, and the scent of street food wafts through the air, a stark contrast to the storm brewing between us. It's almost comical, this juxtaposition of life moving forward while we remain locked in this standoff, as if the universe itself is waiting for us to make our move. I can feel the eyes of strangers grazing over us, curiosity piquing as they recognize the tension, though they can't fathom its depth.

In a moment of inspiration, I take a step closer, narrowing the distance between us. "You know, for someone who claims to be powerful, you sure do like playing games. Tell me, is it exhausting, pretending to be something you're not?"

He sneers, but I can see the flicker of anger igniting behind his mask. "What do you know about power? You've always been just a pawn in my game."

"A pawn can become a queen, given the right circumstances." I lean in, the adrenaline coursing through my veins fueling my defiance. "And you've underestimated me from the start."

The corners of his mouth twitch, perhaps in annoyance or perhaps in disbelief. "You're delusional. The moment you thought you could stand against me was your first mistake."

"And yet here we are," I reply, the satisfaction of my words fueling my resolve. "You may have been the hunter, but I've learned how to fight back."

Suddenly, a group of people brushes past us, oblivious to the storm raging a few feet away. A couple stops to stare, their eyes wide with intrigue. It feels surreal, as if we're performing in a twisted play and the audience is simply waiting for the climax. I can almost hear their collective breath hitching, caught in the tension of our stand-off.

"Don't you want to tell them your story?" he hisses, his voice a low growl. "How I took everything from you, how you begged for mercy?"

My heart clenches, but not out of fear—out of anger. "You think you can scare me? That your twisted narrative will keep me silent? I'm not a victim, and I won't be your scapegoat."

At that, something shifts in him. The facade of confidence fractures just a little more, exposing the desperation lurking beneath. I take a deep breath, feeling a surge of empowerment. "I'll make sure everyone knows the truth. They'll understand who the real villain is."

"Truth?" he echoes, his laughter hollow and brittle. "You think truth matters in this world? It's all about perception, darling. And I've always been the master of it."

I can't help but roll my eyes. "Ah yes, the classic 'look over there while I pull the rug from under you' strategy. How original."

"You think you're so clever." His voice drops an octave, a warning. "But cleverness won't save you from what's coming."

"Neither will your bravado," I shoot back. The back-and-forth feels almost like a dance, each of us testing the other, looking for an opening. I can feel the tension crackling like electricity, each word charged with possibilities, and I know the moment is building toward something inevitable.

Suddenly, a shout slices through the air, pulling my focus momentarily. I turn just in time to see a figure emerge from the crowd, a flash of familiar features that make my heart skip. "Lila!"

My stomach drops, realizing too late that I hadn't expected to see anyone here, least of all someone I care about. As she rushes toward me, her eyes wide with concern, I feel a rush of protective instinct surge through my veins.

"Get back!" I shout, panic rising in my chest. "This isn't safe!"

"Why didn't you tell me?" she breathes, her voice trembling as she glances between us, the atmosphere thick with tension. "I could have helped!"

"No! You can't be here!" My voice rises, desperation lacing my words. "You don't understand what he's capable of."

A flicker of indignation sparks in her eyes. "And you think I can just stand by? You're my friend, and I won't let you do this alone!"

Her determination fuels my anger. I want to scream, to protect her from the danger lurking just beyond our confrontation, but there's something else—an unexpected swell of warmth at her loyalty, even in the face of peril.

"Lila, this is not a game! You have to leave!" I plead, turning back to face him, my resolve solidifying.

"Or what?" he taunts, feigning nonchalance. "You'll fight me off with the power of friendship? Cute."

"I don't need to fight you alone." I square my shoulders, anchoring my resolve. "Lila's right. You've underestimated both of us."

For a brief moment, uncertainty flickers across his face again, the mask slipping just enough for me to see the cracks beneath. He's always thrived on fear, and now, with Lila at my side, I sense a shift in the balance of power.

"Fine," I say, the determination rising in my chest like flames. "Let's end this—together."

As Lila steps closer, her presence beside me transforms the atmosphere, imbuing the charged air with an unexpected warmth. She stands firm, her gaze locked on him, refusing to flinch. I can feel her heart racing, the rhythm a steady drumbeat of resolve that syncs with my own. This moment, this unlikely alliance, feels like a spark igniting a powder keg.

"Lila, I don't want you to get hurt," I say, forcing my voice to remain steady, even as panic churns within. "You don't have to do this. You can walk away."

"Like hell I will," she shoots back, eyes blazing. "You're my friend, and I won't let you face him alone."

The tenacity in her words wraps around me, a protective shield against the looming threat. The world has a funny way of pushing you into impossible situations, and yet here we are, standing shoulder to shoulder against the embodiment of all my fears.

He studies us, amusement dancing in his eyes. "How adorable. Two little girls playing at being heroes." His sneer drips with condescension, but I can see the uncertainty creeping into his posture.

"Heroes? We're more like a reckoning," I declare, matching his bravado. "And you've run out of time."

With that, I take a deep breath, drawing strength from the ground beneath my feet, feeling the city's heartbeat resonate within me. I won't let fear dictate my actions any longer. Together, Lila and I form an impenetrable wall, and as I face him, I realize that this is not just a fight for survival; it's a reclamation of everything I've lost.

He scoffs, feigning indifference. "You think you can take me on? I've built an empire on fear. You're merely a footnote in my grand story."

I can feel Lila's presence beside me, her unwavering loyalty bolstering my confidence. "You may have built your empire, but it's built on lies. You can't keep using people like pawns in your game."

His expression darkens, the facade of confidence crumbling. "What do you know about power? You've always been the sidekick in someone else's story."

The words hit harder than I expected, a flash of doubt threatening to seep into my resolve. But I shake it off. "I've learned from the best. I know how to turn the tables."

In a flash, he lunges forward, a figure of chaos and menace, and everything seems to blur around us. I barely have time to react as he reaches for me, his hand slicing through the air like a blade. "You think you can play with the big boys? You're just a child playing dress-up!"

Lila shouts, "No!" and throws herself in front of me. The world narrows down to a single heartbeat, time stretching like a rubber band as I watch the scene unfold in slow motion.

"Lila!" I scream, my voice slicing through the tension, but I can't reach her in time.

In a heartbeat, she collides with him, a flurry of movement, her body connecting with his like a cannonball hitting a wall. The force of it sends both of them staggering backward, and for a moment, I stand frozen, disbelief washing over me like a cold wave.

"Get back!" I yell, pushing through the shock. Lila and I have come too far to let him win now. My body surges with adrenaline as I take a step toward them, ready to intervene, to shield her from the chaos unfolding before us.

But as I move, I feel a hand grip my shoulder. It's Lila, eyes wide, and she pulls me back, shaking her head. "Wait! We need to think!"

He regains his footing, a glimmer of rage flashing in his eyes. "You think this changes anything? You're still just a distraction, and now I'll make an example of both of you."

The shift in his demeanor sends a chill down my spine. The bravado that once seemed insurmountable is fading, replaced by an urgency I can't ignore. "We need to be smart about this," I whisper to Lila, trying to keep my voice steady despite the rising panic.

"What's the plan?" she asks, eyes darting to him as he circles us like a predator stalking prey.

"Maybe we can use his arrogance against him," I suggest, feeling a flicker of inspiration ignite within me. "He thinks he's invincible. Let's make him think we're scared."

"Scared?" she repeats, a grin breaking across her face. "That's not really my strong suit."

"Act it," I urge, adrenaline coursing through my veins. "If we can get him to underestimate us, it might be our only shot."

"Okay," Lila agrees, her eyes narrowing in determination. "Let's play this like a game of chess."

As he closes the distance, I lean into Lila's plan, letting fear morph into a fierce resolve. I take a step back, feigning hesitation, my breath coming faster as if I'm losing my nerve. "Please," I plead, my voice quavering just enough to make it believable. "Just let us go. You've won. We won't fight you."

He stops, a flicker of surprise crossing his face, and I can almost see the wheels turning in his mind. "Really? You think I'd let you walk away after everything you've done? You're both nothing to me."

"Maybe," I say, forcing a tremor into my voice. "But what if you're wrong? What if we're worth more alive than dead?"

Lila takes a step back, mirroring my retreat. "You've already taken so much from us. Why not let us go? You could show the world how merciful you are."

He pauses, clearly intrigued. I can see the internal struggle playing out across his face. "You think I'm going to fall for your little charade? You really believe you can outsmart me?"

"Believe what you want," I counter, using the moment to my advantage. "But you've never played with someone like me before. I'm not what you think. You've been so focused on your own narrative that you can't see the bigger picture."

A flicker of something—doubt?—crosses his features. I press on, sensing the opportunity. "You want power? Fine. But what happens when all your enemies realize they can take you down? You need us alive to maintain your control."

He hesitates, a taut moment stretching into a silence thick enough to drown in. "And why would I care?" he replies, though his bravado wavers.

"Because you're afraid," I say, leaning into the truth. "Afraid that we might just be the spark that ignites something bigger than you. You may think you're untouchable, but everyone has a weakness."

As I watch his confidence crack, I take a breath, steeling myself for what comes next. "Your empire will crumble without us. You're not as strong as you pretend to be."

In that instant, something shifts in him, a storm brewing behind his eyes. "You think you can manipulate me? You're playing a dangerous game."

I can feel the tension escalating, the air thickening with unsaid words and possibilities. Just as it seems like he's about to react, his phone buzzes in his pocket, a sound that slices through the moment like glass shattering. He fumbles for it, glancing down at the screen, and I can see the blood drain from his face.

"Not now," he mutters under his breath, frustration clawing at the edges of his voice. "Not now!"

It's enough of a distraction for Lila and me to regroup, a fleeting window of opportunity. We exchange a quick glance, and I can sense the plan forming between us.

Before he can regain his composure, I take a deep breath and step forward, heart pounding, ready to seize the moment. "It's over," I declare, determination lacing my voice. "You've lost control."

He looks up, eyes narrowing in fury, but it's too late. The world shifts, the balance tipping as everything hangs in the balance. I can almost feel the ground beneath us trembling, the anticipation building to a breaking point.

"Get ready," I whisper to Lila, the adrenaline surging through my veins. But just as I take a step closer, the unmistakable sound of sirens wails in the distance, echoing through the streets, growing louder with every passing second.

"What have you done?" he hisses, panic now lacing his voice.

"I didn't do anything," I reply, feeling a surge of triumph. "But it looks like your time is up."

With sirens blaring and shadows shifting around us, the moment teeters on the edge, the outcome uncertain. He lunges, desperation etched across his features, but I'm already moving, adrenaline propelling me forward as the sound of chaos looms nearer.

"Run!" I shout to Lila, heart racing as we dart into the fray, the city swallowing us whole. The sirens echo behind us, but it's not just the sound of approaching law enforcement—it's the sound of reckoning, the promise of change.

But in the distance, I see something else—something darker lurking in the shadows, a flicker of movement that sends chills racing down my spine. "Lila, wait—"

Before I can finish my warning,